THE CURSE OF THE
RED DEVIL

THE CURSE OF THE
RED DEVIL

AVA & CAROL
DETECTIVE AGENCY

THOMAS LOCKHAVEN

TWISTED KEY
publishing

2020

First Printing: 2020

ISBN 978-1-947744-51-6

Twisted Key Publishing, LLC
www.twistedkeypublishing.com

Ordering Information:
Special discounts are available on quantity purchases by corporations, associations, educators, and others. For details, contact the publisher at the above listed address.

U.S. trade bookstores and wholesalers: Please contact Twisted Key Publishing, LLC by email twistedkeypublishing@gmail.com.

CONTENTS

I

THE BRIDGE OF DEATH

"You want us to go across that? What am I, a trapeze artist?"

Ava pointed at a rickety bridge made of wooden slats, supported by two large ropes. Normally, traversing a rope bridge wouldn't be a big deal for Ava. However, this particular bridge stretched across a huge chasm, some two hundred feet high, with nothing below her hiking boots but a twisting muddy river teeming with caiman and flesh-eating piranhas.

"I'm pretty sure I wrote that I was allergic to heights…and death on my application," said Ava.

"Look, uhm…," Miquel leaned in to read Ava's iguana name badge, attached to her jacket.

Ava scrunched her nose; he smelled of mosquito repellent and stale sweat. "It's Ava."

"Right. Ava…hundreds of campers have crossed this bridge."

"And are they *still* living?" inquired Ava. "I have big plans for my life and they don't include being eaten alive, or falling so far I run out of breath when I scream. Ahhhhhhhhh. Status check. Yep, still falling, ahhhhhhhh…." Ava kept screaming until she'd emptied her lungs of air.

Carol clapped, and encouraged the others in their small group of campers to do so as well. "Stirring rendition, Aves."

Miquel took off his threadbare Yankees cap and wiped the sweat from his forehead with his shirtsleeve. He squinted at Ava, and then nodded. "Yeah, they're still alive…well, most of them," he smiled, revealing yellowed teeth that looked like old piano keys.

"Relax, Aves," said Carol, nudging her best friend. "He's just messing with you, and besides, look on the bright side. If the bridge collapses, it's only like a…." She peered down into the steep ravine. "…Like a two hundred-foot fall, give or take a foot or two. No way you'd run out of breath. So, you'd definitely be alive when you die."

"That's reassuring. Thanks for the pep talk."

"Glad I could help." Carol grabbed her newly purchased safari hat as a gust of wind swept across the wooded chasm. The bridge groaned and rocked lazily back and forth. Thunder rumbled in the distance. The other campers looked up at Miquel nervously.

Thunder was *never* good news when you were outside, about to cross a flimsy suspension bridge dangling hundreds of feet in the air.

"Okay," said Miquel, looking up at the sky, his demeanor becoming more serious. "No more chitchatting—we've got a storm coming. Marcia," he said, turning to a twenty-something Brazilian woman wearing a camouflage hat and black wrap-around sunglasses. "Make sure we don't lose anyone."

"Not to worry," she nodded. "Okay, everyone," she commanded, "single file, let's go."

"If I become piranha soup," Ava hissed, "I'll never speak to you again."

"Promise?" laughed Carol.

"Ever!" declared Ava.

"All right, Ava," said Miquel, pointing at her. "You lead the pack."

"What?" she asked incredulously. "Why me?"

"Because the best way to overcome your fear is to face your fear. This is an Amazon Adventure Camp. You're going to learn a *lot* about yourself while you're here in the rainforest, and this is your first lesson."

"Can't Carol take my spot? I loathe heights. I actually wrote a paper for school titled *Gravity Hurts*."

"It's true," Carol nodded. "It was poignant."

"Ava, quit stalling. There's a storm coming, and I don't know about you, but I think the rest of your friends would like to cross the bridge before it hits."

"Fine." Ava rolled her eyes—dying, falling, being eaten by carnivorous aquatic life—none of those were at the top of her "Things I wanna do this summer" list. Adventure usually meant eating salad from a salad bar with no sneeze guard…or drinking milk two days past its expiration date. Now *that* was adventure. Plunging to her death…not so much.

"Group leader, set an example," Miquel encouraged brightly. "Come on."

"We're doomed," said Mason, a thirteen-year-old boy with bright green eyes and sandy brown hair. His friend Tony a skinny kid, with a mop of red hair, let out a low laugh.

"Don't worry about them," whispered Carol, giving the boys the stink-eye.

The bridge creaked and swayed as soon as Ava put her foot on the first board. Her heart lurched into her throat and grabbed her windpipe, nearly choking her. She imagined the board beneath her feet cracking—and then, she was plummeting down—down—down into the gaping jaws of a hungry caiman. Chomp. Chomp.

"Ava, you got this. Breathe through your nose," she heard Miquel's calming voice. "And do what I do." He reached out and grabbed the support rope with his right hand, held his balance, and then grabbed the other support rope with his left.

Ava did her best to mimic him. She reached out, gripping the support ropes in a vice grip, her knuckles turning white. *At least if the boards break, I can just hang here, forever.*

"Good," he nodded, encouraging her. "Now loosen your grip, just a little so you can move, and keep your eyes on my back. We'll be across in no time."

Ava didn't speak a word; she kept her eyes zeroed in on Miquel's sweaty back. In the dark recesses of her mind, she was trying to figure out how Carol, her best friend, had talked her into traveling to the Brazilian rainforest—and if Miquel, their intrepid guide, used deodorant, because if the bridge didn't kill her, the noxious odor coming from his shirt surely would.

2
KABOOM

As soon as Ava's feet touched terra firma on the other side of the chasm, she fell to her knees and kissed the ground, swearing she would never leave it again—and that she would plant a forest of daisies and tulips, in honor of solid land masses everywhere.

Miquel stared at her, bewildered. "Is she okay?"

"She *loves* nature," explained Carol. She turned and addressed the group, gesturing to Ava. "We could *all* learn a valuable lesson from her."

"Great job," said Marcia as she followed Lucas, the last of the campers, off the rickety bridge.

Lucas grinned from ear to ear, pushed his glasses up his nose, hiked his shorts to his chest, and threw his fist into the air with a high-pitched celebratory "yah-hoo!"

The celebration continued until his friend Rachael, who reminded Ava of Velma from *Scooby-Doo*, went in for a high-five, missed his hand, and smacked him across the face, sending his glasses flying.

"Oops," Rachael exclaimed.

Lucas picked up his glasses and blew off the lenses, his cheek burning from embarrassment and pain.

"Sorry," gushed Rachael.

"I choose her if we're attacked by a baboon or a creature with fangs," said Ava.

"I second that motion," added Carol. "She clearly has advanced swatting skills."

"Oh Lord," sighed Miquel, obviously wondering what he'd gotten himself into. "Everyone, gather around, gather around," said Miquel, waving them into a tight circle. "Congratulations for making it across dead-man's crossing, guys. That's no easy task. Also great job, group leader." He winked and gave her an awkward thumbs-up.

Ava saw Mason and Tony roll their eyes. "Dead-man's crossing," they snickered.

Boys, thought Ava, *so obnoxious*.

"Base camp just texted me," continued Miquel, pocketing his phone. "Looks like this storm is going to be a nasty one. We're going to have to hustle to make it before it hits."

"How far away is base camp?" asked Rachael nervously. She looked at Marcia, then the sky, then back at Marcia.

"About three kilometers from here. Not far," she answered.

"Three kilometers? What does that even mean?" asked Tony. "Can't you just say the distance in miles?"

"It's about two miles, Tony," explained Elliot from within the hood of his hoodie. "About thirty minutes if we average four miles per hour."

"Rad conversion skills, Elliot," said Carol, clearly impressed. She gave him a giant thumbs-up.

"Yeah, but why not just say two miles?" insisted Tony.

"Very few countries use the imperial system of measurements—miles and feet," explained Elliot. "Most use the metric system."

"Metric system." Mason rolled his eyes. "Ridiculous." His friend Tony nodded his head in agreement.

"Rachael's the group's swatter, a.k.a. Anything Fanged Slayer, and Elliot can be our personal Google, if the internet goes down," laughed Ava.

Carol could see the hint of a smile on his face as he sucked in the compliment like a thirsty sponge. She'd learned on the bus that Elliot's nickname was "Turtle." Every once in a while, his tiny nose would protrude from the depths of his hoodie—but that wasn't very often.

So far, no one really knew what Elliot looked like, except for two almond-colored eyes, a small narrow nose, and lips that slightly puckered outwards from his braces.

Thunder boomed through the ravine like a cannon, making everyone jump. A cacophony of caws erupted from the treetops as a flock of tanagers moved like a rainbow-colored cloud across the sky, seeking safety from the storm.

"All right, we're moving," yelled Miquel. "Stay close!"

Miquel moved effortlessly through the jungle. He cut through thick vines and vegetation with his machete without missing a step. Occasionally, he would throw up his hands, stopping the group to let a colorful snake slither by, or to use the tip of his machete to hold back a branch that was home to a poisonous spider.

"Wandering spider," he called out, pointing to a large brown spider. "*Extremely* venomous." The children slowly scooted by the branch, staring wide-eyed at the deadly spider.

A zigzag of lightning lit up the sky, followed by a loud crackling explosion. Unseen animals shrieked in the trees, frightened by the ferocity of the incoming storm. Carol caught a look of concern in Miquel's eyes. He threw up his hand, bringing the group to a halt.

"What's going on?" Lucas looked worriedly from Marcia to Miquel. "Why are we stopping?"

"Dude is like a walking question mark," scoffed Tony.

Miquel pulled out his phone and began speaking urgently in Portuguese.

"He's calling for backup, from the camp," said Marcia. "They'll take us back to camp by jeep. Everything's going to be okay," she assured. "We get storms all the time."

"It *is* called a rainforest," snarked Mason.

Marcia gave Mason a look that immediately silenced him.

"Give me a roll of duct tape and five minutes alone with that kid," whispered Ava. "I'll turn him into a freaking human burrito. We could leave him for the jaguars, you know, for breakfast."

"Ava Clarke," laughed Carol. "That's dark, even for you."

Miquel pocketed his phone and turned to the group. "Juliana and Gabriel are on the way. We'll keep hustling; we should meet up with them in about ten minutes."

And then it happened. First a scattering of giant, gumball-sized raindrops, and then the heavens opened, releasing a torrential downpour.

"Let's go!" Miquel yelled.

Thunder roared and lightning flashed as the storm descended upon them. Instantly the ground became slick and treacherous. Rain came in waves, thick sheets of water stinging their faces, blinding them. Thunder shook the ground. Lightning exploded in flickering arcs of fury just above the treetops. Animals screeched and howled, scampering through the trees.

Lucas began to sob uncontrollably. Carol grabbed his clammy, wet hand. "Come on, Lucas, you dominated on that scary bridge. You've got this," she encouraged.

Lucas squeezed her hand tightly. "Okay," he replied, more confidently than he felt.

Miquel whirled on his toes, spinning toward the children. "Stop!" he screamed, throwing up his hands. The small group slid to a stop at the edge of a steep ravine.

"Woah," Rachael gasped, "that would have been a nasty fall."

Usually, the rocky gorge would have been easy to navigate by foot, but these weren't normal circumstances. The side of the ravine had turned into a dangerous mudslide. The tiny stream they were supposed to cross to get to camp was now a raging white-capped river, filled with debris.

"There's no way we can cross here. We're going to have to continue downstream to find a safer place," exclaimed Miquel.

"What about the people coming from the camp?" Tony cried out. "How will they know where we are?"

"We can't cross here," explained Marcia. "That means they can't either. As soon as we find a safe place to cross, we'll make our way back to our original meeting spot."

Thunder roared through the valley like a Mack truck; stick lightning sizzled across the canopy.

"I feel like we're in a bug zapper," exclaimed Mason.

"We're so doomed," moaned Lucas. He looked as if he were about to burst into tears again.

"We're going to make it; we're going to be fine. Let's focus on finding a safe place to cross," encouraged Miquel.

The group followed the rushing water, slipping and sliding over wet rocks, roots, and logs. Just when Ava was sure this was all pointless, they came across a downed tree that spanned the width of the creek.

Perfect, thought Miquel as he brought the group to a halt. "Okay, guys, I know it's a lot to ask, but it's the best chance we've got." Lightning crackled in the sky just over their heads.

"You want us to cross that?" Tony cried out. "Have you lost your mind?" The look on his face said, *Yes, Miquel has lost his mind.*

"I hate to say it," Rachael declared, "but Tony's right. That log is soaking wet. If we fall off, we're dead."

"You're going to be okay. You're *not* going to fall. I'm going to make sure of that."

"How?" asked Mason angrily.

"I'm going to cross first. I'll tie a rope to a tree, and Marcia and I will take you over one at a time."

"You're kidding, right? Are you nuts?" pressed Mason.

"Mason!" yelled Miquel hotly. "If we don't cross now, we're going to be stuck in the middle of the jungle, *at night*, without *any* protection. I don't think *any* of us want to be in that predicament. Trust me," he said firmly, staring at Mason.

Mason made a face. "Whatever," he spat.

Without another word, Miquel carefully climbed onto the log, straddling it like he was riding a horse. He placed both hands onto the log, pushed, and slowly moved forward until he reached the other side.

The group stood by, watching in a miserable, wet huddle. Miquel pulled a rope from his backpack and tied it to a tree. He gave the rope a firm yank to make sure it was secure and then tied the other end around his waist like a belt. He straddled the log once again and skootched back to the other side.

"I have a feeling I'm going to be removing splinters from my butt for the rest of my life," whispered Ava.

Carol nodded, agreeing. "Something to do on those long, cold winter nights."

"Listen up." Miquel was addressing the group again. "We're going to cross to the other side, one by one just like I did. I'm going to tie the rope around your waist as an added precaution. Everyone understand?"

A group of soggy heads nodded in unison.

"Group leader," said Miquel, wiping the water from his eyes. "You're first."

Ava's eyes rolled up in her head. She sighed and walked over to Miquel. He quickly wrapped the rope around her waist and secured it with a bowline knot. He gave two quick tugs to make sure it was secure.

"You've got this, Ava," encouraged Miquel.

Ava nodded and picked her way down the embankment to the downed tree. The water rushed at her feet, bubbling and churning like a witch's brew. Usually, during uncomfortable moments, Ava would say something sassy or make a joke—but with one glance up at the soaked children huddled together, she knew she would have to set an example, especially for Lucas. *Wait a minute, is this what maturity feels like? If so, maturity is a bummer.*

"Ava, I want you to straddle the log right behind me. Remember the bridge?"

Ava shook her head "yes," sweeping her wet purple bangs from her eyes. *How could I forget?*

"Follow me just like you did on the bridge, and you'll be across in no time."

Ava nodded again, without saying a word. Inside, she was terrified. The log was muddy and slippery, and even though she had a rope wrapped tightly around her waist, she couldn't help but feel like a worm, dangling on a string above a churning brown river.

She breathed in deeply and, once again, focused on Miquel's back—not feeling the ooze of mud and green gelatinous fungi squishing through her fingers, not feeling the vines and bark tearing and pulling at her legs—just focusing, just moving forward, until she was finally across.

Ava exhaled a sigh of relief as she clambered from the makeshift bridge onto the shore. She turned and gave her fellow campers a big smile and a thumbs-up.

One by one, Miquel led the children across the chasm. Ava reached out, helping to deliver each of them safely onto the shore. When Carol finally stepped onto the shore, Ava grabbed Carol's hand, squeezing it tightly. She smiled at her best friend, her freckled face splattered in a constellation of mud.

"You look awful," laughed Ava.

"I'm just trying to think of it as an invigorating spa day. Fresh rainwater, mud, and humidity to cleanse the pores...."

"More like, death, dying, decay, Bengay fever...," complained Ava.

"It's dengue fever. Bengay is a medical cream, used for topical pain relief."

"Like I said, tropical pain relief. We're in the tropics and we need relief."

"Topical means *on your skin*, not tropical, as in...never mind," Carol exclaimed. "You're exasperating."

"Thank you," Ava replied. "I find your flattery refreshing."

Carol leaned forward and grabbed Elliot's hand, helping him off the log. She heard a muffled "thanks" from somewhere deep within his hoodie.

"He's *so* mysterious," whispered Carol into Ava's ear.

"You need help. The kid looks like a living sock puppet."

"Ava Clarke!" chided Carol.

"Fine, a *mysterious* sock puppet," said Ava, wriggling her fingers in the air.

"Better," snickered Carol.

The tiny group huddled together, waiting impatiently for Lucas to cross. If the circumstances had been different, where people wouldn't *actually* die, it would have been comical to see Lucas squished between Miquel and Marcia, moving like a family of inchworms across the log.

Ava was curious to see if Lucas was going to reenact his celebratory dance. She had hoped Rachael was going to rush forward and make another attempt at a leaping high-five, but instead, he staggered onto the shore, trembling like a frightened puppy.

"I'm a bad person," Ava said guiltily.

"I don't know *what* you did, but accepting who you are is the first step," whispered Carol as she patted her on the shoulder.

The children stood huddled beneath a giant tree, dirty, soaking wet, with their clothing torn. Any exposed flesh was covered in bites and scratches. Rain beat down on them mercilessly, as if trying to pound them into the ground.

"Okay, everyone," said Marcia. "We've made it across! Now all we have to do is backtrack to our crossing point, and we'll meet Juliana and Gabriel there. It's just a little further, I *promise* you," encouraged Marcia.

Mother Nature, however, wasn't swayed by Marcia's impassioned speech. The storm intensified. The rain slashed through the trees like miniature daggers stinging their faces;

thunder boomed, rattling their teeth. The tops of the trees whipped violently back and forth, crashing into one another.

On the ground, things weren't much better. Branches, leaves, and insects fell from the trees onto the children. Their path back to the meeting point was treacherous. Fallen trees and jagged rocks broke through the muddy surface like shattered teeth, their edges sharp and cutting.

"Watch your step!" yelled Marcia, as they picked their way along the water's edge.

A blinding flash of lightning sizzled through the forest like a flaming spear. It struck the tree beside them, sending a massive, fiery tree branch to the ground beside them. The group screamed, scattering into the jungle.

"Stop!" yelled Miquel. "Stop!"

Everyone froze, except for Lucas; he raced blindly through the rainforest, branches tearing at his face, crashing into trees, screaming.

"Lucas!" yelled Carol. She and Ava shrugged off their backpacks, and without another thought, they went racing through the jungle after him. "Lucas!"

"Wait!" Marcia threw her backpack to the ground. "Watch them!" she yelled as she dashed after them.

Miquel stepped in front of the other children. "Stay here," he ordered.

Carol reached Lucas first. She could tell by the way he stood that something was wrong. She took a cautious step toward him. The blood had drained from his face, his lips were pale, and his eyes were glazed over.

"Lucas," whispered Carol. She gently touched his shoulder. "Lucas, are you okay?"

He stood ramrod straight, barely breathing.

Ava joined Carol, gasping for air. "Is he okay?"

Marcia appeared at their side, worried Lucas had been bitten by a venomous spider or snake.

"Lucas," she said gently, taking his hand. "Lucas...are you hurt?" Her eyes followed the direction of his stare, and then she saw it.

The ghastly skeletal head of a demon, impaled by what looked like a twisted spear, the jagged end facing skyward. The skull had eight horns with razor-sharp tips, ruby-red human-shaped eyes, and a mouth full of pointy teeth. A necklace of feathers and bones dangled from its jaw.

Marcia's mouth flew open in surprise. She pointed a shaking finger toward the demon skull, rapidly speaking in Portuguese. She made the sign of the cross over her chest, then pulled Lucas by the shoulders against her.

"It's the mark of the Red Devil," she cried out. "Don't look at his eyes or he will steal your soul!"

Lucas's legs buckled. The demon's eyes flashed red. A bone-chilling scream filled the air as the leaves around the demon's head began to thrash.

Ava looked at Carol. Was it too late? Had the Red Devil stolen Lucas's soul?

Marcia dropped to her knees, scooped Lucas onto her shoulder, and screamed, "Run!"

Ava and Carol didn't need to be told twice. They crashed through the jungle, afraid that the demon would come for them, afraid he would steal their souls.

Moments later, they burst through the underbrush, sliding on their heels, nearly plowing into the rest of the group. Marcia appeared seconds later, Lucas slung over her shoulder.

"What happened?" Miquel asked urgently, seeing the fear in Marcia's eyes. "Is Lucas hurt?"

Marcia's chest felt like it was going to explode. She gasped for air. Miquel helped her lower Lucas to the ground, propping him up against a large rock. Still gulping for air, she tenderly brushed his hair from his forehead. His wide eyes stared back at her, unblinking, his pupils eclipsing his irises.

"Marcia, what is it?" asked Miquel, growing agitated.

She turned, looking up at him. She saw the knife in his hand, the blade slick with rain. "It's the mark of the Red Devil, Miquel…the Red Devil."

Miquel reeled back onto his heels as if he had been punched in the chest.

"Marcia," he asked firmly. "The Red Devil, are you sure? This close to camp?"

"What's going on? Is Lucas all right?" asked Rachael, breaking from the group. "Is he okay?" Her voice trembled as she knelt beside Marcia. A mixture of tears and rain streaked down her face. "Is he going to die?"

"He's going to be fine," said Marcia, gently touching Rachael's hand. "He just saw something that frightened him."

"You said he saw the Red Devil! What the heck is the Red Devil?" Tony cried out, his head swiveling back and forth— expecting the creature to explode from the jungle at any moment.

"Is that what happened to Lucas?" asked Mason accusingly. "There's some kind of creature roaming the forest and you didn't bother to tell us!"

"The Red Devil is ancient Brazilian folklore," said Elliot from the darkness of his hoodie. "It's just folklore."

Everyone grew silent as Elliot continued.

"The locals believe that he roams the forest, looking for human souls. Brazilian folklore says that if you stare into his eyes, then he'll steal your soul, and you'll be under his spell...like a zombie."

"Is that what happened to Lucas?" Rachael asked, her breath catching in her throat. "Is Lucas a zombie?"

"No. No," Marcia replied more strongly, trying to regain control of the conversation before it spiraled out of control. "Lucas will be fine...he's just overwhelmed."

"For real, are we really standing here talking about zombies and devils? This is stupid," scoffed Mason. "There's no such thing as zombies," he said emphatically.

Carol could see right through all of his bravado; Mason was frightened.

"Sure there are," Elliot corrected him, "just not the kind you see in movies and television. There are zombie ants right here in the rainforest. A fungus takes over them and takes control of their brains," explained Elliot.

"So the Red Devil's a giant fungus? Like a walking mushroom? There's no such thing as zombies or zombie ants or demons. Why are you trying to scare us?" argued Mason.

"Okay, enough," said Miquel sternly. "Right now, we need to focus on getting to base camp." Miquel slid his knapsack off his back and handed it to Marcia. "Lucas, buddy, it's your lucky day," he smiled.

He knelt in front of Lucas, and Marcia helped maneuver him onto Miquel's back. "Don't get too used to this," he said over his shoulder.

The group soldiered along the water's edge. They were amazed at the amount of debris that had become a part of the swirling, bubbling brown soup—which, just an hour ago, had been a tiny trickling stream.

Ava watched Lucas bouncing along on Miquel's shoulders. Their eyes met and she smiled at him reassuringly. At least, like it or not, the rain had forced Miquel to take a shower.

3
EAGLE CABIN

The jeep jolted to a stop, snapping its passengers back against their seats. Muddy water sprayed the side of the jeep and splashed onto the windshield. Miquel wasn't kidding; the trip to the camp took less than five minutes.

Ava opened the door, hopped out, and immediately sank ankle-deep into a large mud puddle. Seconds later, Carol slid out the door—and into the same puddle.

Carol inflated her cheeks and blew out slowly. "We made it…. Camp Adventura," she sighed, pointing to a small wooden sign that hung lopsided from a tree branch.

"Our home for the next seven days…. Thank you, Carol," moaned Ava.

"Don't mention it," said Carol, balling the bottom of her hoodie into a wet knot. She squeezed out enough water to fill a Big Gulp cup.

A second jeep screeched to a stop behind them, splashing them with muddy water.

"Seriously?" yelled Ava. "Come on!"

Carol heard a snicker come from deep within the recesses of Elliot's hoodie as he joined them.

Miquel emerged from a large wooden cabin holding a clipboard. He waved the children over to join him on the covered porch attached to the main building.

"Everyone, everyone, please pay attention. I know you're all wet and dirty, so I'm going to make this fast. Once you get your cabin assignment, shower up and meet back here at headquarters in an hour."

"He's definitely an optimist," whispered Ava. "Has he seen my hair?"

"Girls," he continued, "Juliana will be stopping by your cabins to make sure you have everything you need, and to drop off your luggage. Guys, you'll be stuck with me."

"Okay." Miquel looked at his clipboard. "Tony and Mason, Badger cabin, number five." Miquel handed Tony a piece of wood shaped like a badger. A key dangled from its mouth.

"What?" mouthed Tony. He looked incredulously at Miquel, who smiled and pointed to a tiny cabin with a huge friendly badger painted on the door.

Ava snorted, "The Badger cabin."

Mason rolled his eyes as he and Tony made their way through the rain to their cabin.

"Ava, Carol, you're in the Eagle cabin, number one."

Tony stopped in his tracks and held out his hands with a "What gives?" look. "How come they get the Eagle cabin?"

Miquel handed Ava the majestic Eagle key, which she displayed proudly.

"Congratulations, team leader," Miquel smiled, ignoring Tony. "It's our most luxurious cabin."

"Yes!" said Ava, grabbing Carol's hand, running to the famous Eagle suite. "Finally, some good news."

The outside of the cabin wasn't much to look at—a set of worn steps and a small wooden building that looked like it had, at one time, been an unloved tool shed. White paint flaked off the walls, and the green thatched roof was in desperate need of repair. A tiny covered porch extended along the front, upon which sat two very lonely stools.

Carol pointed out where previous campers had carved their initials into the seats. "I never understood why people do that, you know, carving your initials into something. Are they going to return someday and say, 'See, I told you…thirty years ago, I sat right there, on that stool. There's my initials.'"

Ava shook her head. "Probably not," she muttered. She wasn't terribly interested in the stools, nor the exterior of the cabin. She did, however, have high expectations for the interior. After all, they were in the prized Eagle cabin.

"We should probably take off our boots before we go inside," said Carol, noticing the muddy tracks leading up the stairs onto their porch.

Ava agreed. "We have the nicest cabin…we want to keep it that way."

The girls hurriedly flung off their boots, pulled off their wet socks, and hung them on the railing.

"I can't wait to see what it looks like inside," said Carol, balling up her fist in excitement.

"I know," exclaimed Ava. She inserted the key, twisted, and opened the door.

The interior of the cabin was dark, cast in long shadows. Ava felt along the doorframe and wall for a light switch.

"There's the light," said Carol, pointing to the ceiling.

A lone bulb with a silver-beaded cord hung from the center of the ceiling. Ava gave the cord a tug, and the pale bulb flickered to life.

Ava's heart sank as she looked around. The cabin was sparsely furnished. A sagging bunkbed sat against the back wall. To the right of the doorway was a small wooden table and two equally small chairs that reminded Ava of primary school. A tiny window occupied the space beside the door, with the glorious view of the circular dirt driveway.

Ava exhaled. "That smell…. It smells like the Earth threw up in here."

"It just needs to be aired out. It's homey," said Carol, smiling.

A squat dresser with a cracked mirror attached to it occupied the other side of the room. A small card with the words "Welcome to Camp Adventura," signed by the staff members, sat in front of the mirror. A few of the names had been crossed out with new ones written in.

Ava picked up the card and pointed to the names crossed out. "Dead, dead, dead, dead," she declared as she read each name out loud.

"So dramatic," laughed Carol. "After a long, hot shower, things won't seem so bad."

"Maybe so," said Ava, hesitating. "I take it that's the bathroom." She motioned to the back of the room where a decorative curtain hung from a wooden dowel screwed into the wall.

"How quaint," squealed Carol. "Just to show you that I'm a trooper, I'll let you shower first."

Ava pulled back the purple and red privacy curtain and peeked inside the closet-sized bathroom.

"Carol, our toilet looks like a bucket…. Correction, our toilet *is* a bucket with a seat attached to it," said Ava, horrified.

Carol put her arm around Ava's shoulder and leaned in, feeling sure Ava was exaggerating. "Oh, uhm, yes, it is. At least the water is pretty; it's aqua blue."

"Yes…yes, it is," agreed Ava, nodding. "It matches your eyes. And is that supposed to be our shower?" continued Ava. "You realize there's *no* curtain."

"Aha, how chic! How European!" Carol exclaimed.

Inches from the toilet was a small rectangular recess in the floor. The shower floor consisted of a sheet of plastic with a rusted-out drain in the center. A dead roach lay on its back, its legs up in the air as if it were breakdancing.

A black garden hose hung about a foot above their heads from the wall, a rusty spigot just below it. Two yellow washcloths hung from a metal hook at the back of the shower.

"Carol Miller, you have got to be kidding me. We have a bucket for a toilet, a garden hose for a shower, and…," said Ava, looking up, "no shower curtain…and what is this?" Ava picked up a mucous brown clump with copper-colored streaks running through it. "Is this supposed to be our soap? Is it supposed to be that color? It looks like a piece of petrified wood."

"Aves," said Carol reassuringly. "Look, I know this seems like a lot to take in. But we'll adapt; we're adventurers. Do you think Lewis and Clark had it easy? Do you think they had a five-star hotel? No, they slept under the stars. They hunted the land for their food."

"Did they have to pee in a bucket? Who changes that bucket? These are important questions!"

"I'm not sure," said Carol, "but look at the bright side, Aves: We're in the rainforest. You can shower for an hour and you'll never run out of water."

Ava was about to explode when there was a knock at the door. "That better be an Uber driver to take us to the airport," she declared.

Carol was thankful for the interruption. She dashed to the door and flung it open. It smashed into the wall, bounced back, and slammed shut in the woman's face.

"Oops," Carol exclaimed. She opened the door more carefully. A young woman stood on the porch nestled between two pieces of luggage.

"Sorry about that," said Carol. "Sometimes I don't know my own strength."

"No problem! I'm Juliana. I've got your belongings."

"Oh, wonderful. Ava," Carol called out, "our luggage is here."

"Stunning," replied Ava, looking at the tiny dresser at the foot of their beds. "I'll have just enough room to unpack my socks and unmentionables."

Carol grabbed the handles of the duffle bags and dragged them inside.

"I love your hair," smiled Juliana. "Is it always so wavy? My hair has no body at all." She ran her fingers through her shoulder-length brown hair. "Straight and boring."

"I think it's the humidity," laughed Carol. "Makes my hair frizzy and wild like me." She wiggled her fingers at Juliana.

"It's wonderful," Juliana gushed. "So, quick reminder, we'll be meeting at the staff headquarters in about an hour. If you need anything in the meantime, please just let me or one of the other staffers know."

"I think we're goo—"

"Nope, nope, nope," said Ava, appearing in the doorway. "I have a couple questions."

"Oh, wonderful," smiled Juliana. "I love curiosity."

"First, are there any towels? We have two washcloths in our…." She paused, struggling with the word *shower*.

"Oh," said Juliana surprised. "I actually stocked the room myself. I thought for sure I put towels in there."

"Nope," replied Ava. "I found the dinosaur egg—sorry, I mean soap—but no towels."

She followed Ava across the room and peered into the bathroom. "Yes, you have two towels, right there."

"Those are towels?" Ava grabbed one of the so-called bath towels and held it up to her chest; it was the size of an unfolded tissue. "Maybe," said Ava, trying to be as polite as possible, "there is a language difference. Towels are used to dry your body and your hair. A washcloth is used to wash your body." She pretended to dry her body with a towel.

"Yes, of course," said Juliana. "There's no need for a washcloth. The soap is a special blend of clay and herbs; it exfoliates as well as nourishes the skin. My grandmother makes the soap. It's a family recipe dating back seven generations."

Ava bit her lip. She was annoyed and confused, but she didn't want to unintentionally insult the woman's grandmother.

Carol swallowed her laugh, seeing the expression on Ava's face.

"So…this is our towel?"

"Yes," Juliana laughed. "So, any other questions?"

Ava shook her head. At the moment, she felt the less she knew, the better.

"All right then," said Juliana brightly, taking a look at their muddy faces and clothes. "As soon as you get showered and changed, we'll all meet up at the staff headquarters for dinner."

"Oh. Oh, I'm so sorry," said Carol. "What about our dirty clothes? I didn't see a laundry hamper. Is there a community washing machine?"

"Exquisite question." Juliana touched Carol's nose with her index finger. "For tonight, just place your clothes in the corner. Tomorrow, you'll learn how to use a rock and a basin of water to handwash your clothes. It's such a spiritually fulfilling moment for everyone."

"Ah," gasped Carol, placing her hand on her chest. "So organic, it's like heaven."

"Yes, it is," smiled Juliana. She put her hand on Carol's arm. "I can tell you're already connected to the heart of this beautiful country; you're going to have a wonderful time."

Carol's face was beaming when Juliana left. "Did you hear that? My heart is connected to the jungle."

"I wish your brain was connected to reality…. I'm going to take a shower," moaned Ava.

4

THE SHOWER OF DOOM

Ava stepped from the shower, traumatized. She had thought she would be prepared for whatever happened after the bridge of death, traversing the log over the raging river, and the Red Devil. However, *nothing* could have prepared her for the blast of frigid muddy water that sprayed her in the face with the force of a fire hose—slamming her into the wall, drenching her towel. She shook her head dizzily as the cockroach spun in circles over the drain.

Just when she thought the nightmare was over, the hose made a gurgling sound, like a person choking on yogurt—and then the saddest stream of water known to mankind began to slowly trickle from the nozzle of the hose. Ava tried to work up a lather with the fossilized bar of soap, but only succeeded in creating a thin, brownish film on her palms.

She shut off the shower, feeling grimy, and sadly dried herself with her soaking wet miniature towel.

"How do you feel now, roomie?" called out Carol from outside the decorative curtain. "Refreshed? In a better mood?"

Ava whipped the curtain aside and stepped out. "What? What's *that*?" she asked, jabbing at a little plastic baggy in Carol's hand.

"It's my travel bag. Shampoo, conditioner, moisturizer, and travel soap—everything a girl needs."

27

"But, but the 'What to Bring' guide said that toiletries would be provided."

"Are you kidding me? I care too much about these luxurious locks to use just any kind of shampoo. Oh...." Carol's eyes flew open wide. "You used the dinosaur egg soap on your hair. You do know it has all kinds of oils and minerals...."

"So," said Ava, miffed. "What's that supposed to mean?"

"Probably not good for your highlights," shrugged Carol.

Ava's eyes widened. "What do you mean by 'not good'?"

"I'm sure it'll be fine...I gotta get in the shower," said Carol, nodding toward the bathroom. "We're supposed to be at the meeting in twenty minutes."

Carol stepped into the bathroom and swished the curtain closed. "Be out in a minute! Oh, and look on the dresser. My dad gave us matching survivor bracelets; there's blue and green. Take whichever you want."

Can we trade them in for airline tickets? Ava leaned against the wall and waited for the blast of water and the scream...but all she heard was a steady stream of water, and Carol singing something from *The Lion King*—maybe Carol's heart was connected to Brazil after all.

Ava and Carol hurried from their cabin to the staff headquarters. Juliana greeted them at the door with a big smile and directed them out back to the dining area.

"I'm so excited about our first traditional Brazilian meal," chirped Carol.

"I bet you are," said Ava sarcastically. "Please," she gestured, pretending to be at the table. "Another serving of those exquisite beetles for my friend, and oh, yes, that twisty root-looking thing—those are to die for."

Ava's mood perked up immediately when she smelled the fresh aroma of marinated grilled meat and vegetables. A thin woman with silky black, shoulder-length hair was stirring a large pot of delicious-smelling stew.

"Where do you want to sit?" Carol asked. The dining area consisted of three picnic tables connected end to end, beneath a thatch roof and enclosed in mosquito netting.

"How about right there?" Ava nodded. "Across from Elliot and Rachael."

"Sounds good to me," Carol replied, sliding onto the bench. She was about to say hello to her fellow campers when Miquel appeared.

"Okay, everyone, grab a seat." He motioned to the picnic tables. "Tonight, we have something very special for you. Rebecca and her son Daniel have prepared some delicious traditional native Brazilian dishes for you."

Rebecca's face reddened as everyone turned toward her. She was a small woman with a proud face. Sinewy muscles ran up her forearms to her sleeves; it was apparent that she worked hard for a living.

Her son Daniel stared back at the campers, his face a mix of curiosity and resentment. His bleached hair was shaved short on the sides, and the top flopped over his head like a shiny golden wave, covering one of his ears. Carol watched as his eyes passed over each of the campers—she wondered what he was thinking. Probably, *Here we go again, another bunch of spoiled kids.*

"Let's give Rebecca and her son a big thanks for preparing our meal tonight."

Carol led off with an enthusiastic "Thank you!" She elbowed Ava, who let out a whoop, and was joined by the others.

Daniel gathered several plates and placed them onto a large circular platter. He made his way around the tables, serving the hungry campers. Ava didn't realize how famished she was until she took her first bite of *feijoada*, a hearty stew of black beans, vegetables, beef, and pork sausage.

"This is so delicious," Ava exclaimed, not caring that she had a full mouth of food.

"Try one of these," offered Carol, handing Ava a crispy piece of bread, cooked to a golden perfection.

"That's *pão de queijo*," offered Marcia, as she slid onto the bench beside Elliot and Rachel. "It's cheese and bread."

"It's crunchy on the outside," swooned Carol, "and heavenly on the inside."

Ava laughed as a *pão de queijo* disappeared into the dark recesses of Elliot's hoodie.

Everything was going peachy until Elliot asked, "Ava, did you change the color of your hair?"

Ava sat upright and dropped her heavenly *pão de queijo* to her plate. "Carol," she whispered, "*what* is Elliot talking about?"

Carol acted as if she hadn't heard her and continued sopping up the remnants of her stew with a piece of bread.

"Carol," Ava exhaled from her nose like a bull. "I know you heard me; what is Elliot talking about?"

Carol filled her lungs with air, then raised her hand to her forehead. She held the position for a moment, and then let it slowly descend as she exhaled. "Ava, you know we've *always* been best friends…."

"Carol Ivette Miller," said Ava, swelling like a bullfrog.

"Okay," said Carol, putting down her spoon. "Remember when I said I wouldn't use that soap on my hair…?"

A quiet snicker escaped Elliot's hoodie.

"The dinosaur egg soap?" Ava's eyes widened. She slowly ran her fingers through her hair.

"Your hair is green," Carol blurted out. "It's green," she said a little more softly.

"Green? How green?" moaned Ava.

"I don't know," said Carol, "like the color of a pale moss...."

"It's woodsy," offered Elliot. "If that helps."

"It's kind of like the algae that grows on sloths," added Rachael. "It's cute."

"And, perfect for the rainforest," offered Carol. "You'll blend right in."

Ava's chin dropped to her chest. "My beautiful purple highlights," she moaned. "This trip couldn't possibly get any worse."

And then it did. Miquel pulled out his guitar and mouth harp and offered to take requests. Ava died a little inside when Lucas requested Justin Bieber.

5
THE CURSE

Miquel and Daniel lit a circle of citronella torches that surrounded the picnic enclosure, filling the air with a sticky, sweet scent. Darkness had snuck in like a thief, stealing the daylight. The day may have been ending for the children, but for many of the insects and animals living in the rainforest, their day was just beginning. A fascinating array of insects gathered on the mosquito netting, staring at the children—like a cat curiously watching a fish in a bowl.

"That's a lot of insects," said Lucas, staring wide-eyed at the vast array of winged and legged creatures scurrying over the netting.

"That chattering that you hear," offered Ava, "is them looking at us saying, 'Food, food, food!'"

"The citronella oil will help chase them away, Lucas," explained Juliana. "They don't like the smell." She wrinkled up her nose as if she'd smelled something bad.

"Oh good," said Lucas. "I was wondering how I was going to make it back to my cabin."

"We'll make sure that they don't fly away with you," winked Miquel.

"We could hang Miquel's shirts up on posts around the campsite. They're guaranteed to scare anything away," Ava said softly.

"Stop picking on Miquel," said Carol. "He may have a problem."

"Yeah…soap."

Carol gathered up her plate and bowl, stacked Ava's on top, and carried them to a large wooden bin at the end of the table.

"Thank you," replied Rebecca quietly.

Daniel watched Carol closely as she went around the table, gathering other dishes and placing them in the bin.

With Miquel's guidance, the campers moved the picnic tables so they formed a half-moon. He stood between the tables, facing the children. "First, let's thank Rebecca and Daniel again for a wonderful meal."

"Thank you!" chorused the group.

"Sounds like you guys rehearsed that," Miquel joked. "Before we turn in for the night, does anyone have any questions?"

"I have a question," said Mason, brushing his bangs from his face. "What can you tell us about the Red Devil?"

Miquel glanced at Lucas, who sandwiched himself against Rachael. "Okay, I'll tell you the story of the Red Devil. However…." He leaned forward, making sure he had everyone's close attention. "…I want to make it perfectly clear that the Red Devil is folklore. It's not true. There is *no* such thing as the Red Devil, or the Red Demon."

"But Marcia said that she saw…."

"Mason, wait," said Miquel, holding up his hand.

"But she said she…"

"Give me a minute," winked Miquel, "and I think things will make a little more sense. Okay?"

"Okay," said Mason reluctantly.

"Let me start by asking you all a question. Raise your hand if you were taught that Christopher Columbus discovered America."

Everyone raised their hand.

"My teachers taught me the same thing," said Miquel, nodding. "Now we know that he made four voyages, but he never set foot in North America. History books were wrong, teachers were wrong…yet the story continued. Do you know who was the first explorer credited with discovering North America?"

Everyone turned and looked at each other.

"Ask Google," said Ava, pointing to Elliot.

"Giovanni Caboto, also known as John Cabot," Elliot replied without missing a beat.

"That's right, Elliot, very good. John Cabot was an Italian navigator, and he is credited with discovering North America in 1497. The story of Columbus is just one example of a story that sounds factually true…but isn't. So," he smiled, rubbing his hands together. "First, a little history, and then I'll introduce you to the Red Devil legend."

The children nodded eagerly, inching closer to Miquel.

"In 1540, a Spanish explorer named Francisco de Orellana sailed here, to Brazil. He became a famous navigator because he was the first person to sail the entire Amazon River."

"He's famous for sailing a river?" asked Tony.

"The Amazon River," Miquel explained, "is nearly four thousand miles long. It's like sailing across the Atlantic Ocean twice. He also founded the city of Guayaquil, which you all know today as Ecuador."

"But as you all know," Miquel said, looking at the group, "if history has taught us one thing it's—"

"Oh, I know this one," interrupted Ava. "That history repeats itself."

"Yes, true," Miquel agreed. "However, what I'm talking about is conflict. Whenever there is an overzealous new explorer, there's usually conflict with the inhabitants or natives of that land. Captain Orellana had only been in Brazil for a few weeks before he began fighting with the local Tapuyas tribe."

Miquel paused dramatically and leaned forward. "Here's where it gets interesting. In his journal, during his second voyage to the Amazon, Captain Orellana wrote that several men in his crew had become possessed by demons. One of the men on his deathbed whispered the words 'Diablo Rojo' over and over before he died."

"Red Devil," whispered Elliot.

"That's right," nodded Miquel. "The Red Devil."

"Wait, wait," gasped Mason. "You told us there was no such thing as the Red Devil, and now you're saying people died?"

"It's okay, Mason," Miquel smiled, holding up his hand. "It's not what it seems. Let me explain a bit more. That's the point of this lesson."

Mason nodded, settling back into his seat and crossing his arms across his chest. "I'm listening," he sulked.

"One of the last entries in Orellana's journals talked about finding the face of a demon, carved into a piece of wood, with the face painted red—and below the devil's face were the words '*Você foi amaldiçoado pelo Diablo Vermelho.*'"

"What does that mean?" whispered Tony.

"'You've been cursed by the Red Devil,'" replied Miquel.

"I was cursed by Taco Bell once," whispered Ava to Elliot. "It didn't end well."

"But you said that the Red Devil wasn't real, so why did these people die?" asked Mason.

"A devil didn't kill them," offered Carol. "People were behind this...unless devils mark who they're going to kill by whittling a piece of wood and then painting it. That hardly sounds otherworldly or efficient to me."

"I can envision the Mafia sitting around a little table, whittling people they wanna take out. Hey, Tony," said Ava, gesticulating wildly. "Two-Time Rennie has red hair, not brown.... Oh yeah...my apologies, boss. Somebody pass me the brown paint, and make it snappy."

Carol snorted and punched Ava's shoulder. "But for real," she said seriously, "there's no devil behind this."

Rachael nodded in agreement. "It's creepy, but Carol's got a point."

"I imagine a devil more as a 'I point at you and you drop dead' kind of thing," offered Carol.

"Carol's right," said Miquel. "The legend of the Red Devil was created to scare people away from the Tapuyas's land. Most likely, Orellana's men were poisoned by the toxins from a poisonous tree frog. The venom causes its prey to appear possessed or zombie-like...before they die."

"That's crazy creepy," said Rachael, shivering.

"Like how Captain Oreo described his crewmen in his journal," explored Ava.

"How did they get them to eat a poisonous frog?" asked Lucas.

"Great question, Lucas," said Miquel, smiling. "They didn't poison Orellana's men by feeding them frogs. Poisonous tree frogs secrete poison through their skin. The Tapuyas people would collect it and then dip the tip of their blowgun darts into it. As a matter of fact, the golden poison frog has enough poison to kill ten grown men. It's been used here for hunting for centuries."

"Again…creepy," moaned Rachael.

"Agreed," confirmed Lucas, who was pressed up against Marcia's side.

"Were we trespassing on the Tapuyas's land? Is that why there was a Red Devil?" asked Tony.

"No, no, no." Miquel held up his hands, patting the air as if squashing their worries. "Some of the locals here, usually teenagers, think it's funny to scare tourists or adventurers, like yourselves. They play on the fears and superstitions of locals…. Again, remember, Juliana, Marcia, and me…," Miquel tapped his chest, "…all grew up hearing stories of the Red Devil."

"So it's just a prank to scare people?" asked Mason. He smiled. "Good prank."

"Think about it," said Miquel. "Running into a scary-looking mask, in the forest, in the middle of a lightning storm…well, I think it would frighten anyone. Most likely that mask has been there for years, and you guys had the misfortune of stumbling upon it."

"So," said Marcia, standing and addressing the group, "there's no such thing as the Red Devil." She smiled at everyone reassuringly.

Says the woman who yelled that it'll steal our souls…, thought Ava.

"But there are real dangers lurking in the rainforest," Marcia continued. "Poisonous spiders, snakes, caiman, jaguars. That's why you'll need to be alert and follow our instructions."

"Have you ever been attacked by a jaguar?" asked Mason excitedly.

"Not a jaguar," said Miquel, pushing his sock down, revealing a nasty jagged purple scar on his calf. "But I have been bitten by a caiman."

Immediately everyone rushed forward to look at Miquel's leg. "Did it hurt? How did it happen? Did you die?" The children fired off questions at Miquel faster than he could respond.

"If you think this is bad, you should see Marcia's leg. She was attacked by bullet ants," said Miquel, nodding toward her.

"A bullet ant?" ventured Rachael.

"Yes," laughed Marcia, joining in on the sock-lowering fun, showing a series of small white scars lining her ankle.

"Why are they called bullet ants?" asked Mason.

"Because the bite is so painful, you feel like you've been shot by a bullet."

"Oh," he nodded, his eyes roaming his surroundings for crawling critters.

"Carol's still waiting to be shot by Cupid," Ava said. "It's why she cries alone in her room at night. Softly."

Carol smacked Ava on the back of the head. "You're an idiot."

"Ahem," Miquel interrupted, attempting to regain control. "There are *many* things in that jungle that can hurt you…but the Red Devil isn't one of them."

"So," said Lucas, obviously needing closure. "The Red Devil isn't real. It's just something concocted to scare people."

"Yeah, buddy," smiled Miquel. "Sorry to disappoint you."

Lucas's face flushed with relief. In the distance, a loud whooping sound echoed through the night, making everyone jump.

"Howler monkey," laughed Marcia, as another monkey responded.

"Eesh," said Carol, "that thing is crazy loud."

"It's incredible how they communicate," explained Marcia. "You can hear their calls for miles."

"Carol," Ava winked, "sounds like your boyfriend's calling you."

"Ah, funny," said Carol, punching her friend's shoulder.

6
WARNING

The campers all left for their cabins except for Ava and Carol. Ava was ready for a good night's sleep, but Carol insisted that they stay and help Rebecca and her son with the dishes. She felt it was the least they could do.

At first, Rebecca shooed them away, but Carol won her over by asking about her family and where she learned to cook.

Daniel eyed the girls suspiciously as he moved the picnic tables back into a single line. Ava found an old wooden broom and began sweeping. Daniel appeared with a trashcan and dustpan.

"Thank you, Daniel," said Ava, smiling.

"Sure," replied Daniel dryly. It was as if it was too difficult to add any intonation to his response.

Ava squatted and brushed the crumbs into the dustpan and emptied it into the trash.

"You don't have to do this, you know. You guys pay for our services, so...."

"I know," acknowledged Ava, meeting his stare. "There's a big difference between having to do something and wanting to do something. Your mom works hard and made a delicious meal for us—probably the best I've ever had—so this is just a little way for us to say thanks."

Daniel looked at her strangely and then at Carol. For the first time in a long time, he saw a smile on his mother's face. She had Carol's rapt attention. At that moment, something relaxed inside of Daniel. His eyes softened, and he stood gazing at his mother for a long moment. Ava, for the first time in her life, kept her mouth shut.

"What color did your hair used to be?"

"Huh, what?" Ava shook her head, surprised at Daniel's choice of words. "Purple, beautiful luxurious purple."

"Sorry about that. Was it Juliana's famous soap that caused your hair to change color?"

"Good job," Ava smiled. "You don't miss much."

"No, the same thing happened to me," nodded Daniel, running his fingers through his thick bleached blond hair.

Ava snorted loudly, and then covered her mouth with her hand. Carol looked over at them and said something to Rebecca, who burst out laughing.

"I have a suspicious feeling that they are talking about us," said Ava, narrowing her eyes.

Daniel didn't reply. He didn't have to. He was grinning from ear to ear; it felt so good to hear his mom laugh.

Ava slid the trashcan back to the corner where she had found it and leaned the broom and dustpan against a wooden support.

"Rebecca gave us some *pão de queijo* to take back to our cabin," Carol told her.

Ava's eyes grew wide. "*Pão de queijo*." She put her hand to her chest. "My love," swooned Ava.

"It's a family recipe passed down from three generations," Carol beamed. She turned to Rebecca, saying, "Thank you so much again for such a wonderful dinner, and for the conversation."

A beautiful smile spread across Rebecca's face, and she scooped Carol and Ava into her arms and gave them backbreaking hugs. "*Boa noite*, good night," she said, beaming at them.

Daniel spoke briefly to his mom, who shooed them away playfully. "Is it okay if I walk back with you to your cabin?" said Daniel.

"Sure," replied Ava. "Is it dangerous at night?"

"No, not really. We have had some snakes and the occasional jaguar, but we have a guard that patrols the perimeter of the camp at night."

"Oh, cool," said Carol. "Sounds exciting."

"There's a door at the end of the enclosure," explained Daniel. "We can just cut through there."

"Lead on—we're following you," said Ava.

Daniel grabbed a Maglite from a wooden supply shelf, and he flicked it on and off to make sure that it worked. "A lot of creatures like to roam around at night. Do you want to see something really creepy?" he asked, his eyes filled with mischief.

"Sure," said Ava. "Why not?" Carol glanced at her friend like she'd lost her mind.

Daniel extinguished two of the citronella torches, and the jungle was bathed in darkness. He lowered the flashlight and shone it at the grass in front of them. Hundreds of sparkling green stars appeared flickering in the night.

"What is that?" asked Carol. "It's beautiful! Is it the light sparkling off the rainwater?" she asked, moving forward.

"No," said Daniel. "Stay behind me, and I'll show you." Daniel honed in on one of the sparkles—both Ava and Carol gasped at the same time. A huge spider sat in the grass, staring at them.

"It's their eyes reflecting the light from my flashlight," said Daniel. "Cool, right?"

"So all of those sparkles are spiders?"

"Yep," Daniel nodded. "Most of them are harmless, but we can stomp our feet and make lots of noise, so they know we're coming."

"I don't know what's creepier," said Carol, "the Red Devil mask or the spiders."

Daniel remained silent until they reached Ava and Carol's cabin. He looked around and then faced the girls.

"Miquel wasn't entirely honest with you tonight." He lowered his eyes and shifted his feet.

"What do you mean?" asked Ava. "About what? Being bitten by a caiman?"

"No, about the Red Devil."

"He's real?" interrupted Ava.

"Ava," whispered Carol. "Let Daniel speak."

"Sorry," said Ava. "Please continue."

"The mask that you saw in the rainforest, it's not kids playing pranks...and it wasn't meant for you. It was meant for the camp leaders. It's a warning—"

Daniel froze, and suddenly they were bathed in a blinding light—the girls held their hands over their eyes.

"What's going on here?" asked a raspy voice.

"Nothing," replied Daniel, his voice high and unnatural.

"You know you're not to be mingling with the guests. Get back to the lodge."

Without another word, Daniel disappeared into the darkness.

"You two," the man coughed, "it's after curfew. Not safe to be out here—"

"We know," said Carol, cutting the man off. She grabbed Ava's arm and they ran to their cabin, under the watchful eye of the stranger. Carol slammed the door shut and latched it.

"Well, he's friendly," said Ava, looking out the window. The man stood like a statue, shining his powerful flashlight at their cabin.

"Look at it this way," replied Carol. "If he stands out there till morning, we'll have our own personal nightlight."

"What do you think about what Daniel told us?"

"First, I wonder why Miquel lied to us—"

"That's easy," said Ava. "He didn't want to scare us."

"Secondly, why did Daniel say it's a warning to the people who run this camp? This camp has been here forever," mused Carol.

"I don't know," replied Ava. "Your dad researched this camp, right? I'm sure he read reviews and checked it out thoroughly. Maybe we can get a few minutes with Daniel at breakfast tomorrow, because right now we're just guessing."

"Is our nightlight still out there?" asked Carol.

"Yes and no...he's still standing there staring at our cabin...but he no longer has his flashlight on."

Carol pulled the beaded chain connected to their ceiling light, bathing the room in darkness. She double-checked the latch on the door and checked the lock on the window. "I don't know about you," she whispered. "But that guy creeps me out!"

7
WAKE UP

Carol startled awake. Her nervous system was sounding a red alert. She slowly lifted her head and looked at her chest. Eight black eyes stared back at her. A huge creature supported by eight hairy legs stood menacingly on her chest. Carol's eyes moved from the spider's unblinking orbs down to its curved fangs…they were huge.

"Ava!" croaked Carol, afraid to move. "Ava! Help!" she whispered more urgently.

"Ugh," groaned Ava. "What is it?" she asked, leaning over the top bunk, her hair hanging over her face like a mop. "Is that a…. Holy crap, Carol, you've got a tarantula on your chest!"

"Yes…," mouthed Carol.

"One second," shouted Ava, jumping to the floor. "I'll get him!" Ava grabbed a hiking boot, adjusted her positioning to get the best swing, and raised the boot over her head. "This may hurt a little," she warned.

"No!" gasped Carol, stopping Ava mid-swing. "No! Get Miquel. Now!"

The tarantula sensed Carol's movement and slowly moved toward her face.

"Are they poisonous?" asked Ava. "I think I can smash it before it can bite you."

"Miquel," whispered Carol closing her eyes. "Please, Ava, now!"

"Got it! Miquel, I'm getting Miquel." Ava flung open the door and ran outside.

The tarantula took another tentative step forward, moving from her chest to her neck, its prickly hairs tickling her skin as it moved slowly toward her face.

Carol stared at her chin, willing the arachnid to detour from her body onto the bed so she could make an escape. Instead, just like in the movies, two hairy arms slowly appeared on her chin.

Where is Miquel? He probably keeps these things as pets.

Carol held her breath. She felt a gentle tug on her chin, and then eight unblinking eyes appeared on her face, staring into Carol's soul.

"Carol," Ava yelled breathlessly. "We're here!"

Carol lay perfectly still, unable to speak. The tarantula stood on her face, straddling her mouth and nose. *Please don't bite me, please don't bite me.*

"Don't move," cautioned a female's voice.

Who is that?

Marcia's face came into view. She smiled reassuringly at Carol. "Seems like you've found yourself a whiteknee tarantula," she said softly. "They're very common here. Don't move. I'm going to get him to climb onto my hand."

I don't care where he crawls, as long as it's off me.

Carol closed her eyes. She could feel the warmth of Marcia's hand as she gently placed it on her face.

"He's moving," said Ava excitedly, giving Carol progress updates.

Marcia held her hand perfectly still. The giant tarantula slowly crawled onto her palm.

"I've got him now," said Marcia, backing away from Carol.

Carol exhaled, taking in deep breaths. "Thank you," she whispered.

"That is one massive spider," said Ava in awe, moving closer to get a better look. "Carol, you've got to see this thing up close. It's incredible!"

"Think about what you're saying," said Carol, frantically wiping her face and a sheen of sweat from her forehead. "I literally had its foot in my mouth."

"How did you get in here?" Marcia asked the spider, rotating her hand so it faced her. "Did you guys leave the door open, or your window open?"

"No," said Carol. "After Miquel's lecture about snakes and assassin bugs, I considered sleeping in a Ziploc bag. Is it poisonous?" she asked, sitting up, regaining her composure.

"Well, all tarantulas are venomous, but this one's not deadly. If you've ever been stung by a bee, that's pretty much what his bite feels like. Unpleasant, but this little guy won't kill you. You wouldn't hurt Carol, would you?" chirped Marcia at the spider.

"But you're just holding him in your hand," said Ava. "Aren't you afraid?"

"No," she smiled. "Most of the time, tarantulas are docile, and if handled correctly, you don't have any problems. This little guy is a juvenile. When he's fully grown, he'll have a leg span of eight inches—the size of a dinner plate."

"A dinner plate? That's insane," said Ava, trying to imagine a spider that large.

"I'm going to go release him." Marcia paused in the doorway. "I'll have Miquel stop by and check out your cabin to see if he can figure out how this little feller got in here."

"Okay, thank you, Marcia," said Carol. "That was…well, very cool."

"You're welcome," she shouted, waving her free arm as she walked down the steps. "Don't forget, breakfast's in fifteen."

"She is so brave," declared Carol. "I truly admire that woman."

"I'm surprised you didn't use your handy-dandy survival bracelet," teased Ava.

"You laugh," said Carol, admiring her bright blue bracelet, "but someday this bad boy is going to save your life."

"Yeah, yeah, save your speech for the spider," smirked Ava.

8
FOLLOWED

A nervous tingle raced down Ava's spine. They had just begun the day's hike through the rainforest when she had that uneasy feeling that they were being followed. It was that feeling you get when you're sure that someone is hiding behind the shower curtain while you brush your teeth. She looked around at the others, but they all seemed too preoccupied to notice.

Carol was frantically swatting at a cloud of insects swarming around her head. Ava felt a momentary twinge of guilt. She'd put a spoonful of honey in Carol's shampoo. She'd thought it would just make her hair a little sticky. She had no idea that she would attract every insect in the rainforest, but they were drawn to her like moths to a flame.

Mason was busy pulling his sweaty shirt from his armpits, and Miquel was scanning the trees and nearby foliage for wildlife. The rest of the group was talking excitedly to Marcia about the creatures they might see on their adventure. Lucas piped up once again, needing reassurance that there weren't any storms that they might need to know about.

There it was again. A mere flicker of a shadow, silently moving like a wraith along the jungle floor. Ava stopped for a moment, fished her phone from her pocket, swiped to camera mode, and pressed the video button. She raised the camera to her face—pausing momentarily to mourn the loss of her purple highlights.

She'd have to hurry; the group was on the move again. Ava tilted her head from side to side, pretending to take selfies—instead, she watched the screen, searching through the ferns and scattered vegetation for any sign of the mysterious stalker. It took all of her willpower not to react when she saw a shadow dart behind a giant red cedar.

"Got you," she whispered, catching the person on video. Someone was definitely following them. Ava slipped her phone back into her pocket and hurried forward to join the group. She had just caught up to Carol, who was now wearing a shirt over her head to protect herself from flying insects, when Miquel held up his hand for everyone to stop. He raised his index finger to his lips. The group quietly gathered around him.

"Look up there," he said softly. He pointed to a tree, where a monkey with a dark brown head, tan body, and black markings that looked like socks hung upside down by its tail.

"Oh cool," whispered Mason, grabbing his phone from his pocket.

"It's a spider monkey," said Miquel.

Carol shivered at the word "spider."

"It's beautiful," observed Rachael.

"If you weren't looking closely, you'd never see him," said Carol.

"I couldn't have said it better myself," replied Ava, playfully touching her shoulder against her friend's. "Carol," she whispered, "don't react, but we're being followed—and I'm not talking about the insects swarming around your head."

Carol nodded and pointed at the spider monkey. "By who...or by what?" she added, not liking the thought of being stalked by man or beast.

"It looks like a man," whispered Ava. "I shot some video, but he was behind some ferns and then darted behind a tree."

"Should we tell Miquel or Marcia?" asked Carol in a hushed voice.

Ava stared at the monkey, thinking. "Let's let him keep following us. I'd like to get a good picture of him. Maybe one of the guides will recognize him."

Carol nodded. "For now, we'll play it cool."

"Exactamundo," replied Ava, wondering if the spider monkey ever got dizzy hanging upside down by its tail.

The girls rejoined the conversation. Tony was just asking why they were called spider monkeys, and if they actually ate spiders. Carol immediately decided that if the answer was yes, she'd like to have one in her room.

"Great questions, Tony," replied Miquel. Tony swelled with pride, not used to being complimented.

"I've never seen a spider monkey actually eat a spider," mused Miquel, "but that doesn't mean that it wouldn't. These little guys are omnivores. They like to eat fruit, honey, leaves, insects, and even bird eggs."

"But why are they called spider monkeys?" asked Lucas, repeating Tony's question.

"Ah, yes. They're called spider monkeys because they look like giant spiders when they're sprawled out, hanging from branches with their tails and limbs."

"Makes sense," nodded Tony, staring up at the monkey. "Cool name, dude."

"I heard that there are giant spiders called Goliath spiders here, and they're so big that they can eat birds. Is that true?" asked Rachael.

"Yep," nodded Miquel proudly. "There's over three thousand different species of spiders living here in the rainforest. Most are harmless, but there are a few that are deadly."

"Is the Goliath spider dangerous?"

"What do you think, Rachael?" scoffed Mason condescendingly. "If it can kill a bird...."

"Actually," Miquel interrupted, "the Goliath spider isn't really a danger to humans.... Don't get me wrong; it has a nasty bite; its fangs can grow to be over two and a half centimeters long—"

"That means they are about an inch," clarified Elliot, seeing the confusion on Rachael's face.

"Thanks for the conversion, Elliot," smiled Miquel. "The Goliath spider's venom is actually quite weak. The spider we do have to watch for, is the one we saw yesterday," he continued, "the wandering spider."

"Because he's curious?" asked Ava. "Always wondering?"

"Because it's the most venomous spider in the world," explained Marcia.

Miquel laughed. "Wandering spiders are nighttime hunters. They don't build webs; instead they wander the jungle at night looking for prey. Many of them have a really cool feature: red fangs."

"That's really cool," said Lucas.

"Yep," said Miquel, getting into his explanation. "If it feels threatened, it will raise up on its hind legs, lift its front legs straight up, and show off its fangs."

Miquel held out his palm and pretended like his other hand was a spider. He lifted two fingers, and then pretended to attack Rachael. "Gotcha!"

Rachael reacted by slamming her fist into his hand, crumpling his imaginary spider. "Oh my God," said Rachael, grimacing as Miquel looked at his throbbing hand.

"Five years of karate...," she said meekly. "Sorry."

"Highly effective," moaned Miquel. "Highly effective."

"So," laughed Marcia, "two valuable lessons. Stay on the path, and never attempt to surprise Rachael, if you value your life."

"She must be deadly at rock, paper, scissors," joked Ava.

After Miquel's wandering spider speech, the group had no problems sticking to the trail. Mason and Tony even began talking with Rachael, either out of a newfound respect for her martial prowess or out of fear of being crushed like Miquel's hand. They wanted to apologize for their previous rude comments.

Miquel was in the middle of an earnest discussion about leafcutter ants and the fact that they could lift ten times their bodyweight when Marcia pointed excitedly to a large flowering bush. She motioned everyone over.

"Move in slowly," she cautioned. "She'll fly away if you scare her."

"Frighten what?" asked Lucas, staring at the leaves of the towering Miconia bush.

"Right there," said Elliot, carefully pointing to an insect that was hypnotically swaying back and forth.

"It's a unicorn mantis," said Marcia.

"Aves," squealed Carol, "he's got a little horn on his forehead, like a unicorn." Carol already had her phone out, zooming in on the bright green insect.

While everyone's attention was focused on the praying mantis, Ava used the opportunity to scan the jungle. *Nothing*. She slowly turned her head, her eyes probing every shadow…every tree…every bush. Still, there was no sign of the man stalking them.

"Dang," whispered Ava disappointedly.

"Anything?" asked Carol, dropping to the back of the group, joining Ava.

"No," said Ava, shaking her head. "I think we spooked—"

"What the…," gasped Carol, feeling something squishy and cold on her neck.

Suddenly the children were screaming and scattering in all directions. The sky seemed to be literally filled with poisonous snakes, falling onto the campers from the trees. Ava shrieked in terror; she could feel the cold serpent wrapping around her neck. She spun, grabbed the snake by its tail, and whipped it to the ground, stomping on its head. Without a thought, she grabbed a black snake from Carol's hair before turning to help the other children.

Amidst the mayhem, a figure appeared on the path before them—wearing the mask of the Red Devil, his eyes the color of blood. He raised his hand and hurled a cylindrical object at their feet. There was a blinding flash, and then a thick yellow cloud of smoke enveloped them, burning their eyes and throats.

Disoriented, coughing, and gagging, the children crashed into each other, falling to the ground. Miquel and Marcia grabbed them one by one, leading them to safety, away from the smoke and snakes.

"It's okay! It's okay!" coughed Miquel. "The snakes aren't real. They're not real!"

"Use your water to rinse your eyes," encouraged Marcia as she wiped her eyes with her sleeve and then knelt to help the children.

"Why, why would someone do that?" cried Lucas.

"I don't know," said Marcia. She shared a look with Miquel, her face a mixture of anger, fear, and worry. Carol observed the wordless exchange between the two counselors. She had the feeling that they knew more than they were letting on.

Miquel walked ahead of the group and began screaming into his phone, his voice filled with anger. He finished and shoved his phone into his vest.

"Sanchez is on his way," he told Marcia stiffly. "We need to get the children back to camp."

Marcia turned and faced the children. "We're going to head back to camp. Make sure to keep an eye on each other so we can all return safely."

The group trudged along the leaf-strewn path in silence. First, the storms had battled to drive them away, and now a crazed man dressed like the Red Devil had attacked them. What was next?

Carol and Ava followed along behind the group. Carol turned to Ava, tears running from her eyes and snot pouring from her nose. "I'm guessing that's the guy you saw following us," she whispered.

"I think so," Ava whispered hoarsely. She wiped her nose on her sleeve. Unable to stop herself, she looked over her shoulder to see if they were being followed.

"We walked right into his trap," whispered Carol. "He *knew* we were coming."

Ava nodded. "Somebody doesn't want us here…and I don't know how far they'll go to scare us away."

"Remember what Daniel said last night? He said the Red Devil mask we found in the forest wasn't meant for us. He said it was meant for the camp leaders."

"Yeah, I remember," said Ava, waiting for Carol to continue.

"Then why would they attack all of us? Why didn't they just wait for an opportunity to attack Marcia and Miquel?" asked Carol.

"Because maybe…they've been warned already, and they didn't listen."

"Maybe they have…I mean, it would make sense, especially since things escalated so quickly."

Ava thought about what Carol said. They went from finding a mask in the forest to being ambushed; there were no other warnings. "Okay, here's what I think. I think that whoever is behind this doesn't want us here."

Carol stared at her friend expectantly. "That's it? You really dug deep for that one." She stepped behind Ava and began rummaging through her backpack.

"Firefly, what the heck are you doing?"

"Looking for a shovel, in case you have any other deep thoughts. Ah, here we go."

"Very funny. I wasn't finished, you moron. By the way, I didn't see you spring into action and save the day with your survival bracelet. Did it repel snakes? No. Create a shield against teargas? No. Want me to keep going?"

Carol glanced at her blue bracelet and rotated it on her wrist. "It has a compass," she replied smugly.

"Great, we can use it to bore our attackers to death. Besides, that compass is so miniscule you'd need a magnifying glass to even see it."

"Hah. It just happens to have a magnifying glass and a miniature bottle opener." Carol tilted her head to the side. "So who looks foolish now?"

"Take a selfie," scoffed Ava. "Also, if you haven't noticed, we're in the rainforest. Not a lot of bottles around here. When we return to the States, I'm sending you to an afterschool program on smack talk."

"Fine," huffed Carol. "I apologize for assuming you were finished with your explanation."

"Thank you. I accept your apology, and I apologize for making you aware of the worthlessness of your survival bracelet."

"Hey...I apologized," said Carol, scrunching her face.

"So did I!" exclaimed Ava.

"Fine, your hair is green," smiled Carol smugly, "and I don't like it."

Ava's hand flew to her bangs, and her face fell along with her chin to her chest.

"Too soon?" asked Carol, feeling a tinge of guilt.

"Too soon," whispered Ava. "I rescind my offer to send you to a class on smack talk."

Carol bumped her shoulder into her friend's. "Okay, Kermit," she teased, "tell me what you think."

"I think that everyone, including the counselors, were caught off guard by the attack. I also think these threats are somewhat new. Otherwise we wouldn't be here right now."

"Not following you. What do you mean we wouldn't be here?"

"Your dad is the one that found this camp, right? Wait, did I just ask a rhetorical question?"

"Yes, you did, good job," said Carol, patting Ava's shoulder.

"Awesome, I can mark that off my bucket list. All right, we both know that your dad researched the heck out of this place.

Remember, he said he combed through hundreds of reviews and even corresponded with a couple of families that sent their kids here. If there was even a remote chance of us being in danger, he wouldn't have sent us here."

"That's true," agreed Carol. "My dad spent weeks researching this camp."

"And there were no red flags, no warnings from other parents discussing strange men dressed in masks and hurling teargas grenades, right?"

"Like you said," agreed Carol. "We wouldn't be here right now." Carol studied her fellow campers, their heads hung low, coughing, defeated.

"What do you think they're going to do?" asked Ava, following Carol's stare.

"I don't know. It's not much of an adventure camp if there's no exploring. I think the only way we're going to get to the bottom of this is by talking to Daniel."

Ava nodded. "We'll have to figure out a way to talk to him—"

"You guys okay?" Marcia popped up unexpectedly beside them.

"We're fine," Ava answered for the both of them. "Camp Adventura certainly lives up to its name."

"Any idea why he attacked us?" asked Carol. "He obviously knew we were coming," she added.

"I don't have any idea." Marcia shook her head. "Look," she smiled, "I know it has been a crazy couple of days, so from now on Sanchez will travel with us. He was a member of the Brazilian Special Forces. I don't think we will have any more problems with him around," she explained. "Also, Miquel called the local police to file a complaint. Don't you worry." She smiled again as she walked away to join the others. "We'll take care of you."

"How come I feel like the words 'take care of' could get us killed?" whispered Ava.

"We've got to talk to Daniel," said Carol, "before this adventure turns into a tragedy."

9
TRYING TO FIGURE IT OUT

As expected, as soon as the children arrived back at camp, they were told to shower and meet back at the counselor's cabin for a meeting and early lunch. While Carol showered, Ava stared out the window to collect her thoughts. The first thing on their agenda: get some answers from Daniel.

The sky reflected the mood of the camp—mind-numbing gray. Droplets of rain began to fall on the old porch railing, pitter-pattering softly on the roof. Ava suddenly felt exhausted. She eyed her bed, wishing she could curl up beneath the blankets and take a quick nap—after she checked for tarantulas, of course.

A dark-skinned man appeared outside, dressed from head to toe in camouflage like a soldier. He wore a rifle slung over his back, and a machete hung from his belt like a sword. *Must be Sanchez,* thought Ava. *Marcia said he would be protecting the camp.* Sanchez leaned against a jeep, eyeing the lodges wearily. He turned his gaze skyward, and then busied himself rummaging through his jacket pocket. He tapped a box on his hand, then cupped his hands around his face.

"Ah, a cigarette," said Ava softly.

A thick plume of white smoke billowed from his mouth. She shook her head and laughed when Sanchez removed his hat to protect his cigarette from the rain. *Now that's dedication,* thought Ava sadly.

***

It was still raining when the girls left for the meeting. They skirted along the outside of the main cabin and slipped into the screened-in canopy through the door Daniel had shown them. Carol immediately spotted Rebecca and Daniel. They were busily chopping fruit and scooping it into bowls, preparing for lunch.

"I'll be right back," said Carol. "I'm going to say hi to Daniel and his mom."

"Okay," said Ava. She quietly joined Marcia, Miquel, and Juliana, who were deep in conversation with Elliot.

"Are we near a local tribe?" asked Elliot. "I mean, are we encroaching on their territory?"

"No, no," said Miquel, shaking his head. "I don't think it's anything like that. Daniel and Rebecca are from the local village. If there had been any kind of problem, we would have been the first to know. This camp has been a part of the community for nearly twenty years."

Elliot became silent again. Ava imagined that deep inside that dark hoodie, he was deep in thought.

"All right," said Miquel, breaking up their informal meeting. He turned his attention to the campers who had gathered. "Everyone, please take a seat." He waited until everyone was settled before he began.

Carol hurried over and slipped in between Ava and Elliot.

"How'd it go?" whispered Ava out of the side of her mouth.

Carol made a face. "Daniel left as soon as I walked over. He wouldn't even look at me."

"Thank you, everyone," Miquel began. He clasped his hands in front of his waist and inhaled sharply.

"We'll talk about it when Miquel's done," whispered Carol.

Ava nodded as Miquel launched into his speech.

"I know that the past couple of days have been unquestionably horrible," Miquel acknowledged.

"You think?" scoffed Mason under his breath. He made sure it was loud enough for everyone to hear.

Miquel ignored him and continued. "The storm." He unclasped his hands and held them out as if surrendering. "That was just Mother Nature displaying her awesomeness. The Red Devil mask in the woods—we would have never found it had we not strayed from our path."

"What about today? You can't explain that away," interrupted Mason angrily.

"Mason, I know you and the others are upset, and I don't blame you. Everyone is going to have an opportunity to speak in just a moment. Okay?"

"Fine," agreed Mason bitterly. He leaned back and crossed his arms over his chest.

"I don't know if what happened today was a one-time thing. I don't know if it could happen again."

"By 'thing,' you mean being attacked by a crazy man with teargas," scoffed Tony.

"Yes, Tony, that's what I am referring to. At this point, we're going to have to cut off all treks into the jungle so we can guarantee your safety."

Mason threw his hands up and looked at the rest of the children. "What?" he chided. "You've got nothing to say? We paid a lot of money to come here, and now we're being held captive in this camp?"

Miquel's cheeks reddened as he fought to hold back his anger. "No, Mason, you'll only be staying here until we can arrange return flights for you guys. Your parents' money will be refunded in its entirety. I'm sorry," he said softly.

"What?!" yelled Tony, jumping to his feet. "My parents are in Europe. They're not going to be back for a week."

"We'll contact your families and work with them one on one," replied Miquel calmly. "I've hired Victor Sanchez. He is retired Special Forces. The camp will be safe under his guard until we can make arrangements with your parents."

"What about the police?" asked Rachael. "Why aren't they involved? Surely they don't want people harassing tourists in their country."

"We've contacted the police. They are aware of the situation—"

"And?" asked Mason.

"They will be investigating the event. I'm meeting with them this afternoon."

"What if they catch the people responsible for this? Will we still have to leave?" asked Rachael.

"You want to stay?" Tony shook his head at Rachael like she was crazy.

"I'll stay." Mason slammed his fist onto the picnic table, making everyone jump. "You're all a bunch of cowards, afraid of some guy in a ridiculous mask with toy snakes and a smoke bomb. Cowards," he hissed.

"I'm sorry, Mason, but that decision isn't up to you. We are responsible for your safety."

Mason shoved himself back from the picnic table and stormed away into the guides' cabin. Marcia jumped to her feet, racing after him.

"So," asked Rachael, "you didn't answer my question. What if they catch whoever's responsible for this?"

Miquel lowered his eyes. "The chances of that happening…are slim to none."

"But you'll try, right?" she insisted.

Miquel shook his head. "We'll give the police twenty-four hours, but ultimately, like I said, you are our responsibility, and your safety comes first."

Lucas shook his head, his eyes filled with tears. "No," he said defiantly, "this isn't right. This was my one chance to prove to my dad that I was brave. We can't just give up."

"Lucas," said Elliot, "you *are* brave. Tell me, have any of your friends crossed a terrorizing bridge hundreds of feet above a river filled with flesh-eating caimans?"

"No," whispered Lucas softly.

"Have they slid across a log over a raging river, or come face-to-face with a Red Devil?"

"No," smiled Lucas shyly.

"Well, there you have it," encouraged Elliot. "If that's not bravery, Lucas, I don't know what is."

Carol turned toward Ava, and without speaking a word, she already knew what they had to do—find the Red Devil.

10

BATHROOM RECONNAISSANCE

Meet me in the bathroom in five minutes. Daniel reread the handwritten message Carol had surreptitiously slipped into his hand as he passed out bowls of soup.

Carol watched him closely, hoping that he would give her a head-nod or some kind of confirmation, but her heart dropped when he threw the note into the trash.

"He threw the note away," she whispered to Ava.

"Great…. What the heck happened?"

"Maybe someone got to him," suggested Elliot softly. He skootched closer to Carol, which made the tips of her ears burn red.

"Careful," teased Ava. "You may get lost in that hood."

"What do you mean 'someone got to him,' and how do you know what we're talking about? Maybe Ava and I just like whispering."

"We are quite the whisperers," acknowledged Ava proudly.

"Right," said Elliot. "I saw you leave with Daniel the other night, and then you tried to talk to him this morning, but he ignored you. Then, you just handed him a note…which he threw away."

"It was a love note. Carol was bummed that she got turned down by the howler monkeys—"

"Was I that obvious?" moaned Carol, ignoring Ava's rambling.

"No, actually I just heard you tell Ava that he threw the note away. I have amazing hearing."

"Let me guess, under that hoodie, you're hiding massive ears," said Ava.

"Something like that," replied Elliot.

"Can you fly with them?"

"Ava, focus," hissed Carol.

She turned her attention back to Elliot. "Please don't repeat anything we whispered—but the other night, Daniel walked with us to our cabin. He was about to tell us about the Red Devil when the guard chased him away. He said that Miquel and the others weren't telling us everything."

Elliot nodded his head. "I think someone is watching Daniel, or has threatened him in some way. It would explain his behavior."

"I agree," said Ava. "Unless, of course, he was jealous of the howler monkeys."

"Well," said Carol, "There's only one way to find out."

***

Carol quietly opened the door to the women's restroom. There was a sink, a single stall, and a small window. She lowered a wooden latch, then crouched at the bottom of the door, listening. She could hear Miquel's voice. *He must be on the phone,* thought Carol, since there were long moments of silence, and then she didn't hear any other voices.

She caught her breath as a board creaked near the bathroom door, and then a shadow appeared. She quickly unlocked the door and opened it a sliver. She sucked in a gasp of relief. Daniel slipped in, and she secured the wooden latch once more.

"Daniel," Carol started. "What's going on? What happened?"

"Listen." Daniel was visibly shaking. "I can't be seen talking to you."

"Why not?" asked Carol. "We can help."

"No." Daniel shook his head sadly. "This is bigger than you and me."

"You'd be surprised what we're capable of. At least let us know what we're up against."

"It doesn't matter. In a few days Camp Adventura will be forced to shut down. And…my mother—"

"What do you mean 'shut down'?" insisted Carol.

"Shh!" Daniel held his finger to his lips, his eyes open wide. Someone was coming.

He rushed over to the window and shoved it open. The footsteps came to a stop just outside the bathroom door. Carol and Daniel stood still as statues, listening. It felt like an eternity, but whoever it was finally disappeared into the men's restroom. Carol and Daniel didn't move until they heard the scrape of the wood latch sliding into place.

"I've got to go," whispered Daniel urgently.

Carol grabbed him by the arm. "You can't give up."

"It's not giving up. It's called survival—you wouldn't understand."

Daniel's eyes grew cold. Carol felt like she'd been punched in the chest. Her heart felt like it was being crushed.

"Fine," she whispered defiantly. "Maybe I don't, but it doesn't mean I'm not going to try and help."

Daniel was gone. He'd climbed out of the window, tuning her out. She leaned on the sink and stared at her reflection in the grimy old mirror. Maybe Daniel was right. Maybe sometimes you had to give up. Maybe sometimes the risk was too great. A soft *rap rap* on the door disrupted her thoughts. She turned the sink on, washed her hands, and raised the wooden latch.

"Hi, Juliana," said Carol, opening the door for her.

"Hi, Carol," said Juliana, smiling awkwardly. "What a mess," she said, shaking her head. "I feel so sorry for you guys."

"It's okay. I actually learned quite a bit...but I'm more worried about Camp Adventura, and you guys. What's going to happen to Daniel and Rebecca?"

Juliana shook her head. "They're from a small village.... This was their livelihood. Daniel's dad died when he was seven, and he's been helping his mom here ever since."

Carol nodded sadly, not sure what to say next.

"Get back to your friends," smiled Juliana. "Things will work out how they're supposed to work out." She gave Carol a hug, then shooed her away.

When Carol returned to the canopy, everyone was gone except Rebecca, who was busily sweeping beneath the picnic tables. Carol offered to help her, but she simply responded with "Your friends are waiting for you in your cabin."

Carol stood for a moment, watching Rebecca. What a difference one day had made. Rebecca had spent the last twenty years taking care of other people. Carol set her jaw; it was time that someone took care of her.

II
OPERATION FIND OUT WHAT'S GOING ON

Ava was just about to slam Elliot in the chest with a hiking boot when Carol walked into the cabin.

"Ava Clarke, what the heck are you doing with my boot?"

"You're back! Elliot and I were reenacting your tarantula attack. I was just about to show him how I launched into rescue mode—but now you've obviously ruined it, simply by being here."

"Okay, well that's nice. I'll have you know that while you were in here creating your little fictional melodrama, I was gathering important information and putting my life at risk."

Ava turned toward Elliot. "And she's calling *me* melodramatic? I hope you're not expecting a pay raise."

A chuckle emanated from deep within Elliot's hoodie. "Are you guys always like this?"

Carol thought for a moment and then smiled. "As far back as I can remember. We've actually been friends since we were three."

"That's really sweet," laughed Elliot.

"Okay, okay," said Ava, throwing her hands up. "Enough of this memory lane stuff. Carol, please stop wasting our time and tell us what you found out on your spy mission."

Elliot swung his feet around and sat on the edge of Carol's bed.

"Our assumptions were right—"

"You cry softly into your pillow at night because no one loves you?" Ava interrupted.

"You're exhausting…," sighed Carol.

"I'm sorry, please continue, Care-bear."

"Someone got to Daniel. He's afraid to tell me what he knows. He said that it was bigger than all of us."

"What the heck is that supposed to mean?" asked Ava.

"He thinks we don't have the resources necessary to remedy the situation," explained Elliot.

"Very well put," said Carol.

"Do you think that it's someone within the camp, and that's why Daniel's scared to say anything? Or, or…," said Ava, snapping her fingers. "Why do people usually try to scare people away?"

"Because they're trying to hide something," responded Carol and Elliot in unison.

"But what could they possibly be hiding?" Elliot asked. "We're in the middle of the rainforest."

"Carol and I think the attacks are something new," Ava replied.

"Why's that?" asked Elliot.

"Because there's nothing online about any problems here. All we could find were glowing reviews from parents."

"Well, that's about to change…. I have a feeling that Mason and Tony are going to do a lot of damage," Elliot commented.

"Yeah," agreed Ava. "I think we'd be in a lot better shape if we knew who we were up against. Is it just one guy, or is it a whole group of people?"

"But if Daniel's not talking, and Miquel and Marcia aren't talking…," Elliot started.

"Ava and I will figure it out," Carol said.

"And how exactly do you plan on figuring it out?"

"Like we always do, reconnaissance."

"I hear what you're saying," said Elliot. "But it's not computing. Can you add a few more descriptors?"

Ava held up her hand and paced back and forth across the room. "You may not know this about Carol and me, but we are highly trained investigators. Our powers of observation are boundless—"

"Anyways," interrupted Carol, waving Ava aside. "Remember where we found the Red Devil in the jungle?"

Elliot nodded, "How could I forget?"

"That's where we need to start looking. Whoever is behind this, can't be far from where we found the Red Devil. They're using it to scare the locals away."

"It's a perfect plan," said Ava. "The locals believe that the Red Devil will steal your soul if you look into his eyes. Heck, even Carol and I were afraid it was going to steal our souls." Ava turned to Carol, "Well, she was, not me. I think all of this demon stuff is childish."

"So, just to be clear," summed up Elliot, "you two want to go snooping around in the rainforest looking for clues so you can track down a crazed maniac that hurls rubber snakes and teargas at children."

"Exactly," beamed Ava.

"And you think they're going to just let you waltz out of your cabin into the woods? Plus, don't forget they've got Sanchez watching over the cabins now."

"Yeah, I know," said Carol. "That's the major hiccup right now. We need some kind of distraction—I keep wracking my brain about it."

"Leave that one to me," said Elliot confidently. "Anyone crazy enough to try to sneak out of a cabin guarded by an armed soldier, and then go traipsing through the jungle at night, deserves my help."

"You think you can distract Sanchez?" asked Carol.

"I've got the perfect plan. Cabin check is at 9:30—you guys be ready at exactly ten o'clock. Trust me, I'll keep his attention long enough for you to sneak out."

"Do we want to know?" asked Ava.

"Let's put it this way.... Everyone is guaranteed to be surprised."

12
ELLIOT GOLD

A row of powerful spotlights illuminated the horseshoe drive in front of Camp Adventura. The rain had stopped, and now light rippled on the surface of the newly formed mud puddles. Two gasoline generators hummed in the night, powering the newly placed spotlights.

Ava crouched in front of her window, peeking outside. Sanchez was perched atop a jeep, a rifle lying across his legs. The orange tip of his cigarette blazed in the night.

"Hopefully Sanchez doesn't have to chase anyone. His lungs probably look like beef jerky."

"Gross," laughed Carol. "Ew, think about it, maybe that's what jerky is made out of."

Ava snorted. "Thanks for the visual."

"Three minutes till ten," announced Carol quietly. "Let's hope Elliot's right about his plan."

"He's a smart kid, and he looked pretty confident. Well…I think he looked confident. He stays hidden in that hoodie, so who knows."

"He's so *mysterious*," gushed Carol. "Such an enigma!"

"Oh my God," Ava groaned. "You're absolutely hopeless, you know that?"

"Someday you'll grow a heart, and you'll know what it feels like to be in love."

Ava rolled her eyes and sighed. "I hope not."

Sanchez flicked his cigarette into the sky. Ava imagined a miniature asteroid burning through the darkness, plummeting to the earth—an explosion of sparks flying away on impact. "And that's what happened to the dinosaurs," whispered Ava softly.

"What?" whispered Carol.

"Nothing, don't distract me. I'm being vigilant."

Sanchez leaped from the jeep, rested his rifle on the hood, and stretched his arms above his head. He moved his hips from side to side like a metronome.

"He's up and moving," said Ava, her face glued to the window. "I've either just witnessed his weekly calisthenics routine or he's about to break into the Macarena."

Sanchez walked from one end of the horseshoe-shaped drive to the other. He fidgeted in his pocket for a moment, and then lit another cigarette. For a long moment, he stood motionless, his head cocked to the side, staring into the jungle.

"Is he looking this way?" asked Carol.

"Nope, he seems to be focused on something in the jungle."

Carol quietly unlocked their door and opened it just a sliver. The loud drone of the generators and the smell of gas filled the room. She crawled across the floor and joined Ava beneath the window. "Remember, as soon as Sanchez is gone, we bolt for the side of the cabin where he can't see us, and off into the woods."

"I'm all over it," whispered Ava.

A door slammed, making both girls jump. They could hear the sound of feet pounding downstairs—and then a voice. Elliot's voice, loud and shrill. He raced behind the two jeeps, screaming, "It's in my room! It's in my room!"

Sanchez dashed over to him, shouting at him in Portuguese and pointing back to his cabin.

The girls could see Elliot pleading with him, jabbing his finger at his cabin. Miquel came racing out of the guides' house, dressed in polka-dotted boxers and a T-shirt—with a machete in his hand.

Elliot was waving his arms hysterically, yelling about something in his cabin. Miquel had his hand on Elliot's shoulder. Sanchez looked around suspiciously. And then it happened. Elliot whipped back his hood. Miquel gasped. Sanchez gasped. Ava and Carol gasped. All the creatures in the jungle gasped.

Miquel and Sanchez stepped back as if punched in their chests, their mouths hanging open. Ava and Carol turned and looked at each other, and then back at Elliot.

"Elliot is a girl?" Ava's mouth hung open in disbelief.

An avalanche of golden hair appeared from beneath Elliot's hoodie. She shook her head from side to side as if she were filming a shampoo commercial. Elliot wasn't just a girl; she was a world-famous teen singer—she was Elliot Gold!

"That's—that's Elliot Gold," whispered Carol. "Right there…." Her finger jabbed at the window.

Elliot dramatically gestured toward her cabin again, and this time the men bounded after her like puppies. Elliot was right; she'd given Ava and Carol the perfect opportunity.

"Go!" whispered Ava urgently. "Go!"

13
THE KNEE OF DOOM

Ava and Carol raced through the darkness, stealthily making their way along the perimeter of the camp to the main trail.

"I can't see a thing," whispered Ava. "It's suffocating." She patted her front pocket, making sure her phone was still there.

"Me either, but we're still too close to the camp to use our phones' flashlights. We can't risk Sanchez seeing us. As long as we stick to the main path, we'll be fine. Just don't touch anything," Carol added.

"Great—can I breathe?" Suddenly a hand slapped over Ava's mouth, and another grabbed her arm. Instinctively, she whirled and struck out with her knee. She felt the impact of the blow and heard the gasp from the attacker as the air rushed from their lungs. She coiled her body and was just about to smash her elbow into the assailant when she heard a faint wheezing voice.

"Ava, it's me…," a voice gasped. "Daniel."

"Daniel?" whispered Ava, surprised. "What are you doing here?"

"Following you two—what else?" he groaned.

"Sorry about the knee," offered Ava. "But you can't just grab people in the dark."

"Lesson learned," he squeaked. "Give me a moment…. I think you kneed my stomach into my lungs."

Ava couldn't see him in the inky blackness, but she imagined he was hunched over, hands on his thighs, fighting to breathe. She felt badly for slamming him in the gut, but she also felt proud of herself.

"Okay," he whispered.

"You better now?" asked Carol.

"Yeah, she got in a lucky shot, but I'm fine."

Ava rolled her eyes. "You're just lucky I didn't crush your head with the elbow-of-doom. Half a second later, and we wouldn't be having this conversation right now."

"Okay, seriously, what gives?" asked Carol. "Were you spying on us? You weren't followed, were you? Because we made sure we—"

"Me, followed? Hah!" Daniel scoffed. "As if. I've been keeping my eyes on you two. I figured you'd do something stupid, that's all."

"I can't see in the dark," whispered Ava. "But my guess is you were pointing at Carol when you said that."

"You said that you couldn't get involved," said Carol, an edge to her voice. "So, we decided to take matters into our own hands."

"I'm sorry," said Daniel, backing down. "I'm angry at myself.... I should be the one out here trying to figure things out, not you guys."

"Well, you kind of are. No one asked you to follow us out here," said Carol, a little more softly.

Daniel acknowledged Carol's peace offering. "So," he said, trying another less abrasive approach. "Do you guys have a plan?"

"Of course," declared Ava. "You're not dealing with novices. We'll track down the clues, figure out who's behind the attack, and then Big Brain over there will decide how we proceed."

"I see…," Daniel said, nodding. "Well, then you're going to need an experienced guide. The jungle is dangerous enough during the day…. At night, with all of the animals roaming about, it can be terrifying."

"Oh, we'll be fine," Ava replied sarcastically. "We've got miniature compasses and bottle openers."

"The survival bracelets have more than that," said Carol defensively. "They have a little flint to start fires, string…."

"Are you two always like this? Bickering at each other?"

"Are you insinuating something about our relationship?" asked Carol.

"Nope, I'm just thinking this is going to be a long, long night."

14
AN OLD FRIEND

"Wait a second," Daniel whispered for the eightieth time.

The girls came to a stop behind him. Daniel stood perfectly still, his eyes closed, listening to the familiar sounds of the rainforest. He'd done this many times as a young boy, exploring the jungle with his ears, listening to the shrill burst of insects, the rustling of branches as monkeys scampered through the trees. A smile spread across his face. This was his home, this was where he found inner peace, and tonight the jungle was alive with life—vibrant, radiating with energy, just as it should be.

"All right," he said softly. His voice carried with it a comforting security. "It should be safe to turn your flashlights on now."

"Thank God," whispered Ava. She quickly fished her phone out of her pocket before he changed his mind. "I feel like I've lost a pint of blood to these miserable mosquitoes." She tapped the flashlight app on her phone. The beam illuminated Carol's face, blinding her.

"Why...?" Carol whispered angrily. She threw her hand in front of her eyes. "Thanks, Ava. Now all I can see is glowing blobs."

"Sorry...my mistake. Woah, you should *really* see all of the insects swarming around your head. It's amazing."

"I think I may have seriously misjudged you guys," said Daniel, shaking his head.

"I'm pretty sure he's saying we've exceeded his expectations," said Ava out of the side of her mouth.

"I'm *sure* that's what he's thinking," replied Carol.

The trio walked along the leaf-strewn trail. Their flashlights shone through the darkness, revealing pie-sliced wedges of jungle. All around them, unseen creatures scampered, scurried, and slithered along the forest floor.

"Look!" Ava exclaimed as the path widened. Dozens of rubber snakes lay strewn across the ground. Seeing them lit up by the harsh, white light from their phones made the girls feel foolish for being tricked by the toy serpents. "I can't believe we were fooled by fake snakes. They don't even look real," said Ava.

"Yeah, but combine it with a crazy man in a demon's mask, an unfamiliar environment, and teargas, it's easy to see why everyone panicked," said Carol.

"They used fishing line," said Daniel. He held up a pointed bamboo stake, wire knotted around the top. "They used a trip wire," he explained. "Someone stepped on the trip wire, slipped the string off this little hook, and…." He pointed his flashlight upward. "That's where the snakes came from."

An open net hung above them. A few rubber snakes dangled, trapped in the netting.

"Here's the irony," said Ava. "I bet they bought the snakes from Amazon, to hide in the Amazon."

"Good one, Aves," laughed Carol. "So…whoever ambushed us knew that we would come this way."

Daniel nodded. "Of course, this is the main path to the river and observation point. The guides use it with every group that comes to Camp Adventura."

"Oh yeah," Carol remembered. "Miquel was taking us to the observation point.... Unfortunately, we were ambushed before we could get there."

"Is that where we're heading now?" asked Ava. "To the observation point?"

"Yes, we're going to the stream, and then we'll follow along the shoreline until we reach where you saw the Red Devil," stated Daniel.

"I hope we can remember where we saw it," said Ava. "We were all running, and not really focusing on—"

"I remember two things," Carol interrupted. "Lightning hit a tree, and a huge limb fell to the ground."

"That's right," said Ava. "That's what spooked Lucas."

Carol nodded. "Then, when Marcia brought him out of the jungle, she laid him against a rock shaped like a turtle."

"Perfect! I know that rock," smiled Daniel. "Should be a piece of cake."

Right, thought Ava, *a cake filled with spiders, snakes, and jaguars*.

***

The Camp Adventura observation deck wasn't much of a deck. It consisted of an old battered sign and a rectangular swath of land. A series of logs outlined the border of the nonexistent deck.

"I'm confused," said Carol. "Usually a deck is...well, a deck. This is just part of the riverbank, surrounded by logs."

"Yes.... It used to be, but it had to be rebuilt after every storm," Daniel explained. "Miquel got tired of rebuilding it, so he decided to just section off an area with logs and call it the observation deck."

"It's definitely got that natural feel to it," said Ava.

"All right, so now we just follow the creek upstream, right?" asked Carol.

"Yep, just make sure you stay away from the edge." Daniel aimed his flashlight at the water. The girls could see two glowing orbs staring back at them.

"You've done this trick before. Spiders, right?" teased Ava.

"If their eyes were that big, they would be some massive spiders. Those eyes belong to a caiman," said Daniel softly.

"Oh...creepy," whispered Ava. "Do they eat people?"

"They'll eat anything they can fit in their mouth," said Daniel matter-of-factly.

"Well, that means your head is safe, Care-bear," snickered Ava.

"Seriously, you need some new material," said Carol, turning to follow Daniel.

The trio carefully picked their way along the bank of the stream. Creatures of all shapes and sizes jumped, splashed, and slid into the water as they approached.

"You know what's weird?" said Carol, thinking out loud.

Ava bit her tongue.

"How loud these frogs croak. I mean they're surrounded by predators, yet they sit there on the rocks and shoreline, announcing their location. It's like they're saying, 'Here I am—come eat me. *Croak.*'"

"It's incredibly romantic and poetic," Daniel declared. "They're willing to die to find a mate."

"Poetic? They inflate their throats and make a belching sound. I do that every time I eat Taco Bell. There is nothing poetic or romantic about that," said Ava.

"Maybe not to you," said Daniel, leaping over a moss-covered log. "But to me, it's magical."

"There's the turtle rock!" said Carol excitedly.

"And the tree limb that was struck by lightning!" Ava pointed to a large charred tree branch.

"So, this is where you guys entered the jungle?"

"Yeah," replied Carol. "The tree limb fell, and Lucas bolted into the jungle. Ava and I ran in after him, and found him staring at the Red Devil mask, like he was in a trance."

"All right," said Daniel, his voice serious. "We're going off the path, so stick to me like glue. Don't touch anything, and don't grab anything. Got it?"

"Got it," the girls chorused, falling into line behind him.

Daniel proved to be quite skilled. He navigated effortlessly through the jungle. Several times he stopped the girls and pointed out unseen dangers. The most stunning find was a bright yellow snake coiled around a branch just above their heads.

"Eyelash viper," whispered Daniel, shining his light on the serpent. "They're not aggressive, but they'll bite if startled or threatened."

"It's beautiful," said Carol softly. "Why is it called an eyelash viper?"

"It has a row of scales above its eyes that make it look like it has eyelashes."

"Oh, cool. He's gotta be poisonous, right?" asked Ava. "I mean, he's bright yellow, and his last name is Viper," she reasoned.

"Oh, yeah, a bite from this guy could definitely kill you. He's got a unique venom that attacks both your nervous system and cardiovascular system at the same time." Using his flashlight, Daniel stood on his toes and carefully raised the branch a little higher so the girls could pass beneath.

Carol's mind flashed back to when the rubber snakes had fallen on her—a cold chill ran down her spine.

"How far do you think you guys ran through the jungle before…." His voice dropped to a whisper. "Never mind." Daniel stared transfixed by the twisted, evil face of the Red Devil. "That thing is hideous," he said shakily.

"Red Devil, meet Daniel. Daniel, meet the Red Devil," whispered Ava, motioning toward the demon.

"Don't move any closer," Daniel warned. "There may be trip wires." He knelt and shone his flashlight around the base of the twisted wooden pole. "Wait here," he said softly. He was just about to step away when he turned back toward them. "Remember, don't touch anything."

Daniel made his way through the darkness. The light from his flashlight bobbed through the forest like a gargantuan firefly. He stopped and then shimmied up the trunk of a large walking palm. Hanging on by one arm, he placed both feet on the trunk, compressed his body into a ball, and then, using his legs, he jumped to another tree.

"He's like Indiana Jones and Spider-Man all in one," whispered Ava.

Carol nodded silently. *Why is he jumping from tree to tree like a spider monkey?*

Daniel leaped to another tree and then slowly lowered himself to the ground behind the Red Devil's mask. The glow of his flashlight shone through the eyes of the demon's mask, giving them a sinister red glow. There was a sudden flash of steel, and then Daniel stepped back, a fistful of wires in his hand.

He cautiously maneuvered around the Red Devil and made his way back to the girls. When he was just a few feet away, he stopped and pointed out two trip wires leading into the jungle. They were attached to small wooden stakes, identical to the ones they had found from the snake ambush.

"Interesting." Daniel knelt and dropped the wires to the ground. He leaned forward on his hands and knees, studying something hidden in the underbrush.

"What is it?" asked Carol.

"Stay back!" he cautioned. He grabbed a stick and tapped it on the trip wire. There was a sound like a sword cutting through the air, and then the tiniest of thuds. Daniel pointed to the tree beside them.

A small wooden dart, the length and thickness of a pencil, protruded from the trunk. Daniel removed the dart and held it up for the girls to see. "A poison dart. You see that gooey liquid that looks like syrup? That's most likely venom from a poison tree frog."

"Wait, you mean that thing could have killed us?" asked Ava. "I'm extremely valuable."

"I doubt it's lethal. Most likely it's a strong, uhm, what's the word…it makes you see things?"

"A hallucinogen? It makes you hallucinate?" offered Carol.

"Yes!" exclaimed Daniel, snapping his fingers. "Or it can put you in a trance like a zombie."

"Wow, these guys are evil. We're going to have to be extra careful," said Ava, scouring the ground for more trip wires.

"Exactly," agreed Daniel, picking up the wires and electronics he'd pulled from the Red Devil. "Well, at least the first part of the mission has been successful. I've saved us from a poisonous dart, and I've removed that thing's brain." He motioned to the Red Devil.

"Well, that's certainly gonna ruin his day," laughed Ava.

"What is all that stuff?" asked Carol, gesturing toward the tangle of electronics in his hand.

"Uhm, batteries, a bunch of wires, and this thing." He held up a small rectangular box. "I think it's a miniature camera."

"Woah, that's pretty sophisticated," said Ava.

"Yeah, it looks like it has a motion detector that triggers a camera and a bunch of other gadgets."

"Like the eyes flashing red, and the branches whipping around?"

"Probably," said Daniel.

"At least they got my picture while my highlights were still purple, not this hideous green," said Ava, blowing her bangs from her face.

"You know," said Carol, putting Ava on auto-ignore, "the mask doesn't look so frightening when it's not shrieking and its eyes aren't flashing."

"True," agreed Ava. "I'm curious, Daniel. What does that little sign say, below the mask?"

"'Death to those who look into my eyes,'" replied Daniel in a sinister voice.

Ava snorted. "Was that you, trying to sound ominous? Death to those who look into my eyes." She wriggled her fingers at him.

"You know, they should post that warning in multiple languages," suggested Carol. "I mean, if you're gonna kill someone, you should at least have the decency to kill them in their own language."

"It's just a warning. But you saw the effect that it had on Marcia and Miquel. We've all grown up with the legend of the Red Devil."

"Yeah, we get it," said Ava. "It's to scare off the local tribes."

"My grandmother still makes the sign of the cross whenever he's mentioned. Okay, enough jibber-jabber. Stay close to me and mind the trip wires."

15
THE BEAUTY OF TAPE

"Down, down," whispered Daniel. The trio quickly crouched behind a cluster of ferns covering a downed log. In the distance, a pale-yellow light shone between the trees.

"Is that their camp?" whispered Ava.

"I'm pretty sure," Daniel said quietly. "I wish I had a pair of binoculars."

"Maybe Carol's survival bracelet can help," Ava snickered.

"The only thing that would help right now would be a zipper," Carol said under her breath.

"What's that shadow, just past the ridge?" asked Ava. "Do you see it?"

"That's the Cobra Pequena—"

Ava looked at him, confused. "Tiny cobra?"

"It's a river. It twists through the jungle and flows all the way to the Amazon."

"And from the Amazon," added Carol, "to the Atlantic Ocean…."

"Yep," nodded Daniel. "Perfect for smuggling."

"Do you think this is what it's all about? Smuggling?" asked Ava.

"I'm pretty sure. The rich will gladly pay thousands for exotic birds from the rainforest."

"So, if you're right, can't we just contact the authorities?" Ava asked.

"Not without proof."

"Let me guess," whispered Ava, "they bring money into the local villages, and it helps the economy?"

"No." Daniel shook his head. "Sadly, men like this, keep the money for themselves—and pay off the police and other officials to look the other way. Ordinary people like me and my mom…well, we're of no concern to them."

"Okay, then, let's sneak into their camp, dig up whatever we can, and turn over the evidence to the police," Carol suggested.

The trio carefully trekked through the jungle to the edge of the Cobra Pequena. The water was murky and thick with mud from the heavy rains.

"Do you hear that?" Ava asked.

"Generators," Daniel replied.

"It looks like a military base," said Carol. "I can see four— what is that? Sheet metal?"

Daniel shrugged.

"Okay, four sheet metal structures, a jeep, a bunch of crates—"

"And some cages over there." Daniel pointed behind the largest building.

"Don't forget the boat." Ava pointed to a camouflaged speedboat bobbing in the water. A huge floating pallet the length of two automobiles was attached to the back of the boat.

"They must use it to transport the animals to a larger boat. There's a huge port at the mouth of the river—hundreds of boats come and go every day," Daniel explained.

"Great. Now that we're here, I have one important question. How are we supposed to get across the river?" asked Carol. "That water is filled with caimans and piranhas and who knows what else."

"And leeches," added Daniel. "*Lots* of leeches."

"Leeches?" stammered Ava, her face turning green to match her highlights. "No one said there were going to be leeches involved."

"Everyone makes such a big deal out of leeches. They don't hurt, they're just annoying to deal with," said Daniel.

"What do you mean they don't hurt? They bite you and then suck your blood out! It's disgusting!" exclaimed Ava.

"It doesn't hurt because they secrete some kind of numbing saliva when they bite you, so you don't feel it—and when they're full, they fall off," Daniel explained.

"I'm sorry," Ava declared. "I know it may seem strange, but I like to keep my blood where it belongs: in my body!"

"Oh my God, just stay out of the water," said Daniel matter-of-factly. "And you'll be fine."

"Again," Carol said. "I ask, how do you propose we cross the Cobra river?"

"I've got that covered. I built a lightweight raft for us."

"You built a raft?" Carol looked at him suspiciously.

"Why are you looking at me like that?" Daniel shrugged his backpack off his shoulder and quietly unzipped it. He reached inside and pulled out what appeared to be two garbage bags duct-taped together.

"That's your raft?" Ava looked from Carol to Daniel, then back to Carol.

"Yes, we just find a straight strong branch, run it vertically across, and put it through the two duct tape loops at each end. Then we find five strong sticks, run them horizontally across the boat, and run them through the loops."

"That's not going to float," said Ava, crossing her arms. "I'd rather take my chances trying to swing on a vine like Tarzan across the river than get in that thing."

"Seriously, Daniel, you want us to float across a river named after a deadly snake, on a homemade raft...," Carol said.

"Yes, I do it all the time."

"*Really?*" asked Carol, narrowing her eyes.

"Okay. Okay, fine. I built a raft once."

"And...," prompted Carol.

"And what?" asked Daniel defensively.

"And...?"

"It sank," sighed Daniel.

Carol shook her head. "Ava, you got any ideas?"

"Why don't we just use that?" asked Ava, pointing to an old canoe lying in a tangle of roots and overgrowth.

"Because it's broken and filled with holes," replied Daniel. "That thing wouldn't last a second."

"Stop being so dramatic. You were about to have us sail across the river in two trash can liners. Compared to that, this is a cruise ship."

"Can't we patch the holes? Is it really that bad?" asked Carol.

"Only one way to find out," said Ava as she began working her way down the ravine to the shoreline.

Just as Ava crouched to lift the boat, she felt something smack her in the back of the head. "Ouch, what the heck is the matter with you?" whispered Ava angrily, wheeling around to face Daniel.

"Sorry," he apologized, holding up his hands. "I couldn't yell, and I had to get your attention…quickly."

Ava glared at him, waiting for an explanation.

"This canoe's been here forever, which means it's probably…someone's home."

Ava looked at him for a moment, and then the realization of what he was saying hit her—like a stick.

Daniel searched the shoreline for a moment and then returned with a large tree branch. He carefully slid the thick part of the branch under the bottom of the boat and flipped it over. Curled up in a pile of dead leaves was a slender black and gold snake.

"It's a cobra," shrieked Ava.

"It's not a cobra, Ava. It's a whip snake."

"Is he venomous?" asked Carol, keeping her distance.

"No, he's more afraid of you than you are of him."

"How would you even know that?" Ava shook her head. "Every time I hear that, I'm waiting for the follow-up: 'Nope…I was wrong. He wasn't afraid of you at all.'"

"Is she always like this?" Carol's look confirmed his suspicion. "All right, little guy," said Daniel as he gently prodded the snake with a stick. "Move on."

The snake hissed once more in a last act of defiance and then slithered away.

"I feel bad that we took his home," said Ava.

"He'll find a new place. There's plenty of downed trees. He'll be fine." Daniel quickly checked the rest of the canoe. Other than a couple giant beetles and an old sock, the canoe was clear.

"I call dibs on the sock," snickered Ava.

"Here," laughed Daniel, dangling it in front of her.

"It doesn't look too bad," said Carol, inspecting the hull of the boat. "I see three holes that need patching. Any ideas what to use?"

"Leaves and mud?" offered Ava. "Soles from our shoes? A rubber tree?"

"Duct tape," said Daniel.

"You seriously think that duct tape is going to work?" asked Ava.

"It's actually a great idea," said Carol. "There was an episode on *MythBusters* where they made an entire boat out of duct tape. They sailed it in the ocean for like seven hours."

"Were the people actually *in* the boat?"

"Yep," nodded Carol.

"Wait, you would sail in a boat *completely* made out of duct tape, but you wouldn't sail in mine?"

"Sorry, Daniel, not a chance," blurted Carol.

"I agree with Carol. I think yours had some serious design flaws."

"Geez, thanks," Daniel grumbled.

"Not all of us are boat builders. It's important to know your strengths," said Ava.

"Guys, seriously, do we really want to waste time talking about which boat is the best, or do we want to get on with our mission?" Carol asked.

"Fine," agreed Daniel, somewhat moodily. "Here's the duct tape."

The trio got to work patching the holes, and then with the remainder of the tape, using branches and sticks, they created a pair of rudimentary oars.

"Actually, it's not bad," said Daniel, giving the boat a once-over. He looked out over Cobra Pequena and then let his eyes travel up the riverbank to the campsite. It was eerily quiet.

"She's ready," announced Carol, pulling the boat toward the shore. "Let's go ruin some bad guy's day!"

16
WREAK HAVOC AND DESTROY

Daniel eased the boat into the murky water and held it in place while Ava and Carol clambered inside.

"We're good," said Carol, giving Daniel the thumbs-up.

Daniel crouched low and gave the boat a mighty shove, and then, with perfect timing, he jumped and landed in the back. The canoe wobbled precariously from side to side, and for a moment it looked like it was going to capsize. But to everyone's relief, it righted itself.

"If anyone finds my heart, let me know," moaned Carol. "I think it just shot out of my chest."

"No kidding," said Ava, over her shoulder. "Maybe a little warning before you go all *Titanic* on us."

"Yeah, yeah, yeah," said Daniel under his breath.

Ava lowered her makeshift paddle into the inky black water and began rowing with long, even strokes. She'd kayaked a lot with her parents in Livingston, so for her, crossing a fifty-foot river was a walk in the park.

"I think the best place to beach the boat is that shallow spot. Do you see it, right there by that twisty tree?" asked Daniel.

"I see it," replied Ava softly. She pulled hard on her left oar, turning the boat ever so slightly to the left. A black caiman surfaced, stared at her curiously, and then crossed silently in front of the bow of the boat.

"Aves, you may want to paddle faster," said Carol, her voice tinged with worry. "I think we've sprung a leak...or two."

Ava glanced down at her feet. Two inches of water sloshed around the bottom of the canoe. "Seriously? The people on *MythBusters* sail in the ocean for seven hours, and we can only make it three minutes?"

The slow leak became a miniature geyser. Daniel transitioned from guiding the boat to joining Ava, paddling furiously toward the shore.

Carol dropped to her knees and began scooping water out with her hands, but it was useless. The water was almost level with the top of their canoe. She was pretty sure she saw leeches mixed in with the muddy water. "We're gonna—"

Just then the boat lurched to a stop, pitching everyone forward. The bow of the boat had become entangled in vegetation, just shy of the shoreline.

"Land ho," announced Ava. She leaped from the boat into the shallows, and then sank ankle deep in brownish ooze. Ignoring the grotesque, wet sucking sound coming from her feet, she reached out and helped Daniel and Carol out of the sinking canoe. Seconds later, all that remained of the boat was a cloud of bubbles.

"Great," exhaled Carol, staring at the spot where their boat had disappeared. "How are we supposed to get back across?"

"Uber?" offered Ava. "Do they have an Uber boat service?"

"I think that joke's run its course," replied Carol dryly.

"They have a speedboat," Daniel pointed out. "My guess is the keys are hidden somewhere in it."

"The very definition of overkill," stated Carol. "Taking a speedboat across a fifty-foot river."

"Why are you complaining?" asked Ava, pulling her feet out of river muck. "If it makes you feel any better, we still have our oars. We can just row across."

"I'm just saying if things go badly, we're going to need an escape plan. We need options."

"That's fine, and I agree. However, Daniel and I have both made two great suggestions," Ava retorted.

"Guys, can we have this discussion somewhere else? We're kind of out in the open here. Maybe we can strategize behind that fallen tree," Daniel pointed to their right.

"Good idea," agreed Carol.

The trio climbed the small embankment, and then, running, crouched low. They ducked behind a large cluster of ferns growing on a mushroom-covered log. In the distance, banks of spotlights powered by car batteries illuminated the perimeter of the camp.

"I don't see any guards," said Daniel quietly. "But it's hard to be sure with all the shadows."

"I don't either," whispered Carol.

"Which building do you think they're keeping the animals in?" Ava asked.

Daniel took a moment to scan the rickety sheet metal buildings. "I'm guessing it's that one."

He pointed to a large rectangular building with a massive exhaust fan in the back. Small ventilation slits were cut along the roofline and filled in with wire mesh. The outside walls were lined with metal cages and wooden crates.

"Makes sense," agreed Ava. "See all of those antennas on the other building? I'm betting they have some sort of radio for communicating with their cronies."

"Cronies?" mouthed Carol. "What, are we in the 1970s?"

"And…," continued Ava, "someone wears supersized tighty-whities." She pointed to a makeshift clothesline that ran from the front of the building to a wooden pole with a spotlight mounted on top. "Could be a third option for an escape," she suggested. "I'm sure Daniel could twist that thing into another boat or a parachute."

"I'm not touching those things."

Carol sighed. "Guys, it's gonna be morning, and we're still going to be sitting here behind this log."

"Sorry," said Ava. "Did you come up with a plan yet, Big Brain?"

"I did. I actually came up with two. Plan one: we sneak into the building where they're holding the animals captive. We shoot video, collect evidence, and then rush it back to the police."

Daniel frowned and crossed his arms over his chest. "Let me just say it right now, I'm not a fan of plan one."

"I thought as much," said Carol. "And that's why I created another plan—which I must admit is currently a work in progress. It's also more challenging," she added as a disclaimer.

"Oh my God," moaned Ava. "Get on with it. I'm about to buy a welcome mat and build a home in this log. I've already named it."

"Fine," Carol snapped. "We get videos and pictures just like before. We *have* to do that," she stated, staring down Daniel. "Once we have our evidence, Daniel and I will free as many animals as possible, while you…," she turned to Ava and smiled, "…wreak havoc on their camp."

"I like the sound of 'wreak havoc,'" Ava grinned. "If we survive this mission, I'm creating a T-shirt that just says 'Wreaks Havoc.'"

"And for the coup de grâce," smiled Carol, rubbing her hands together. "We steal their boat to get across the river, and then we sink it."

"Oh!" Ava's mouth flew open. "Can we burn it?"

"What? No!" exclaimed Carol. "We might set the jungle on fire."

"Woah," said Daniel, grinning. "I hope that I never make you two mad at me."

"So...I guess we've decided then." Carol smiled knowingly.

"Plan two," grinned Ava, punching her fist into the palm of her other hand. "Wreak havoc and destroy."

17
CAPTURED

Ava, Carol, and Daniel flattened themselves against the sheet metal building that housed the trapped animals. The exhaust fan whirred noisily above them.

Ava peeked around the corner of the building. "Ah!" She threw her hand over her mouth, muffling a scream. A giant centipede crawled toward her, its creepy-crawly legs marching in unison.

Daniel grabbed Carol by the arm, pulling her away from the wall. "It's a...."

"Scolopendra," Ava whispered, catching her breath. Miquel had warned them about this particular venomous creature that could grow to be up to a foot long and was known to eat baby birds and bats.

"Eesh!" Ava shuddered as the insect crawled away. "I'd take a *tarantula* over that thing any day."

Carol nodded. She had to agree with Ava, having come face-to-face with a tarantula. The Scolopendra was much creepier.

"Come on," Daniel motioned, disappearing around the corner of the building. "We've got to hurry."

The trio crept quietly along the wall, their shadows bobbing beside them. Daniel held up his hand, signaling everyone to stop. He stared at the bad guys' lair for what seemed like an eternity, and then, dropping to his hands and knees, he gestured for the girls to follow him to the front of the building.

"It's locked," moaned Daniel, pointing to two giant doors secured by a thick chain.

"I don't see a lock," Carol whispered. "It looks like the chain is just wrapped around the latches."

"Oh, you're right," Daniel nodded.

"Talk about being overly confident," muttered Ava, crawling toward the door. At that exact moment, a floodlight came to life, enveloping them in light. The trio froze, expecting the worst. Ava held her breath, listening, afraid to turn around. Luckily, the camp remained silent.

"Motion detectors," whispered Daniel, pointing to two floodlights mounted just below the roofline. He shook his head, angry at himself for not seeing them.

"That was sloppy," said Carol, agreeing with him. "We should have seen them."

"It's nobody's fault," declared Ava. "We just need to be a little more careful. Daniel, before I touch anything...do you see any other alarms or traps?" she asked.

Daniel painstakingly examined the doors, looking between, above, and below for any type of magnetic connector or anything that could trigger an alarm. "I don't see anything," he said softly. "But...."

"I know," said Ava. "We'll have to take our chances."

Ever so quietly, she unwound the chain from the door handles. Carol helped to make sure that the two loose ends didn't clang together. In unison, they slowly lowered the heavy chain to the ground.

"That was intense," whispered Carol. Cold sweat dotted her forehead.

Ava nodded and grabbed the handle, slowly opening the door. Instead of an ear-splitting alarm, she received a pungent blast of stale air, smelling like old socks and manure. "Holy moly, breathe through your nose," she warned, stepping inside.

Carol followed Ava inside. Her mouth dropped open in disbelief and her eyes filled with tears.

At least fifty magnificent birds were crammed into tiny wire cages lining the walls. Two incubators sat on a table, filled with eggs. A series of heat lamps connected to car batteries warmed a box of hatchlings.

"This is horrible," breathed Ava. Her first impulse was to race around the room and free all the birds. But she knew whoever did this needed to be stopped, or this atrocity would just continue.

"We should just let them all go," Daniel whispered, balling up his fists in anger. "We should release them!"

"We will," Carol said decisively. She put her hand on Daniel's shoulder. "I promise you, we will. But we need to stick to the plan. These men need to be stopped, and without our evidence, it's going to be their word against ours."

Daniel shrugged her hand off his shoulder. "Okay," he nodded.

Carol pulled out her phone and began filming. "They can't even move their wings," she whispered, her voice breaking.

"There must be a dozen blue macaws," said Daniel, turning in a circle. "There's scarlet macaws," he said, pointing to a beautiful group of fiery red birds. "Hyacinth ones…. There are at least half a million dollars' worth of birds in here, maybe more."

"Well," said a smooth voice, making the girls and Daniel jump. "Someone knows their macaws. Perhaps I can find a place for you on my team." A shirtless man wearing a Chicago Cubs baseball cap and an evil smirk stepped into the doorway. His chest and arms were covered in tattoos and scars.

The trio shrank back into the shadows. Ava scanned the walls and ground for anything she could use as a weapon.

The tattooed man scrutinized Daniel like a bug under a microscope. "I can help you." The man gestured to the cages. "I'll make more with this one haul than your entire village will make in five years, groveling like beggars."

"You're disgusting," said Daniel. "I'd rather starve." He sneered and spat into the dirt.

"'Disgusting?'" laughed the man, amused. "I'm more like an opportunist. I find rare gems," he gestured to the birds. "I delicately mine them, and I sell them for a profit. Much like your American friends, like Indiana Jones, no?"

"You're confusing imagination with reality. You're taking living, breathing creatures from their homes...and selling them," hissed Carol angrily. "It's inhumane."

An evil smile spread across his face. "Oh, your concern...." He clutched his heart and fell backwards. "So inspiring. I'll repent right now and turn from my evil ways," he laughed, mocking her.

"You should. If you had an ounce of kindness, you would release them."

"If you're *so* worried, perhaps you should talk to your friends," he sneered. "After all, they're why I do this—you rich foreigners crave the exotic. You spend millions a year on my feathered treasures."

"Do you realize these animals are going extinct because of people like you? What happens to your little treasure trove when they're all gone?" asked Carol angrily.

"I'll be rich! I'll actually make more money, my darling. The less there are, the more valuable they are. Scarcity brings top dollar, my dear.... You'll learn about that when your mommy and daddy are no longer paying all your bills for you."

"What the heck is he talking about?" asked Ava angrily.

"The less there is of something," explained Carol. "the more valuable it is. Supply and demand."

"Smart girl, but not smart enough to mind your own business. Enough of this mindless bantering. Raul, come here." The tattooed man moved to the side. A thin, dark-skinned man wearing a black tank top and camouflage pants skulked into the dark room.

"Take my guests and lock them in the supply room. By the time anyone finds them, we'll be long gone and they'll be somebody's dinner."

"You got it, boss." The man smiled and pushed past the ringleader.

"Oh," said the man in charge, "I almost forgot. You won't be needing your phones. And Raul, make sure you crush hers," he said, pointing to Carol. "She's quite the little photographer."

"You heard him," yelled Raul. "Give me your phones." He ripped Carol's phone from her hand, threw it to the ground, and then stomped on it, grinding it into the ground with the heel of his boot.

"Oops," he smiled, revealing three teeth hanging on for dear life. "You'll never get those memories back." He held his hand up to his mouth as if saying, "Oh my."

Ava and Carol glared at the men. They'd dealt with dangerous individuals before. "Patience," whispered Carol, seeing the rage in Ava's eyes.

Daniel obviously didn't get the *patience* memo. When Raul reached for his phone, Daniel slammed his fist into his nose, sending the man reeling back into a row of cages. The frightened birds squawked and fluttered wildly.

Daniel whirled toward the ringleader and charged him. He dropped his shoulder, expecting to slam into the man's stomach. Instead, at the last second, the man deftly stepped aside, and Daniel crashed into a mountain of a man, who was at least as wide as he was tall. Daniel crumpled to the ground, moaning.

"Meet Franco the Bull," laughed the ringleader. "Okay, boys," he said, turning on his heel. "Lock them up."

18
TRAPPED

The girls walked solemnly behind Franco the Bull. He'd effortlessly thrown Daniel over his shoulder like a sack of potatoes.

"At least we solved the mystery of the tighty-whities," whispered Ava.

Carol raised her eyebrows and nodded. "For sure."

"Put me down, you oversized cow!" screamed Daniel, pounding his fists into Franco the Bull's back.

"He's like a toddler," laughed Franco.

Not wanting to be left out of the fun, Raul shoved the girls harshly from behind. Ava figured he was probably in a really bad mood after being slugged in the nose by Daniel.

"Your new home," laughed Franco, dropping Daniel from his shoulder.

Daniel hit the ground with a thud. The impact knocked the wind from his lungs. He tried to wriggle away, but Franco put a foot on him, pinning him to the ground.

"You're like a fish," he laughed. "What's the matter, you don't like your new home?" He leaned forward, putting more weight on Daniel's chest.

"Ohhhh," moaned Daniel, struggling to breathe.

Franco searched around in his pocket for a moment and then turned to Raul. "I need the keys." Raul tossed him a set of keys. Franco deliberately fumbled the catch, dropping them onto Daniel's face. "Whoops, sorry." He picked them up and then took his time sorting through them, one by one. "Where are you hiding?" he mumbled in a singsong voice, pretending not to notice Daniel squirming beneath his foot.

"Aha!" He unlocked the door to the supply shed and flung it open. "I hope you're not afraid of the dark," he laughed. He picked up Daniel by the seat of his pants and flung him head over heels into the darkness.

"What are you waiting for?" growled Raul, shoving the girls. "Get inside."

Ava bit her lip. She wanted to drive her heel into Raul's gut, but she knew Franco the Bull would be on her in a second. He was big, but he was fast. *Patience*, she told herself, *patience*.

The girls stumbled into the darkness. Carol tripped and smacked her head against something jutting out from the wall. A cluster of glowing stars filled her vision. She kicked out in frustration.

Ava fared a bit better, crashing into what felt like a stack of car tires.

"Good night," laughed Franco, slamming the door shut. Seconds later, they could hear the sound of the padlock being snapped closed.

"Daniel, Carol," whispered Ava. "Are you guys okay?"

"Yeah," said Daniel angrily. "I'm fine." Ava could hear him pulling himself to his feet.

"You okay, Carol?"

"Yeah, I may have a permanent dent in my forehead, but if I wear bangs, hopefully no one will notice."

"I hear guys dig dented foreheads, so you should be fine," Ava teased.

"I don't get it. How did they catch us?" asked Daniel. "Silent alarm?"

"Who knows," said Ava. "It could have been anything. Right now, we've just gotta figure out how to get out of here."

"Everything is ruined," said Daniel. "They crushed Carol's phone, so we have no evidence, and we're trapped in this stupid shed."

"You can't give up. This is just a tiny setback," Carol said reassuringly. "Plus, I did get pictures and videos, not only of the birds, but also of the men."

"In case you didn't notice, we're locked in a storage shed, they took our phones, and they crushed yours...remember?"

"First," exclaimed Carol, "I have no plans on staying in this poorly constructed monstrosity that does not even deserve to be called a shed. My dad's an architect, and this is embarrassing. Secondly, have you even heard of the Cloud?"

"Of course. I may live in the jungle, but it's not like I'm Tarzan. Although, I do have a crush on a girl named Jane at my school."

"No," agreed Ava. "I don't see you as Tarzan. More like George, George of the Jungle."

"Anyways," continued Carol, ignoring Ava. "All of the video and pictures I took were instantly uploaded to the Cloud."

"So you got everything?" Daniel asked excitedly.

"Yep, even a video of the ringleader and Raul."

Carol couldn't see Daniel in the darkness, but she could tell that his mood had improved from hopeless to semi-hopeless.

"Ava, do you have your survival bracelet on?" asked Carol.

"No," replied Ava. "The color clashed with all of my hiking gear."

"Seriously?"

"Seriously," stated Ava. "I'm not kidding."

"Oh my God," moaned Carol. "You would be lost without me." She held up her wrist. "It has a flashlight built into it."

"Well, I didn't think I would need a flashlight, okay? I mean, we had flashlights on our phones...until Raul took them." Ava could envision Carol rolling her eyes in the dark.

Carol pressed a button on the side of her survival bracelet and instantly the room was filled with light.

"Look, that's what you banged your head on," said Ava, pointing to the handles of a massive wheelbarrow.

"Great...to know." Carol slowly rotated her wrist-light, exploring the shed. "There's gotta be something we can use to get out of here."

"All I see are tarps and old cages," said Daniel. "And there's no way through those doors—they're locked tight."

"Okay, first," declared Ava. "We're in a poorly constructed shed that looks like it was put together by third graders, so if push came to shove, I think I could take that wheelbarrow and use it as a battering ram on those doors."

"Yeah, like that wouldn't draw any attention," scoffed Daniel.

"I said if push came to shove. So far there's no shoving necessary because you two are completely unaware of the obvious."

"Enlighten me," offered Carol, searching the shed for a way out.

"Has anyone noticed that we're standing on a dirt floor?"

"Dirt!" said Carol excitedly, rotating her wrist-light toward the ground.

"Exactly," nodded Ava. "Find what you can—we're digging our way outta here."

Carol slowly turned, illuminating the interior of the shed, taking inventory. There was the old wheelbarrow, a bunch of wire cages, and a stack of tires.

"I've got what I need," said Ava, brandishing a jagged piece of scrap metal.

Daniel braced his foot against a broken cage and pried a wooden slat loose. "Here." He handed a piece of wood to Carol, and then broke off a piece for himself.

It's rudimentary, thought Carol, eyeing the piece of wood. *But it's better than nothing.*

"A little light over here, if you don't mind," whispered Ava.

"On it." Carol placed the wrist-light on a cage and aimed it downward, so it lit up the back wall of the shed.

Daniel dropped to his knees beside Ava and began scraping away at the soil. The earth was soft and made for easy digging. The worst part was the constant skittering and wriggling of bugs that hurried toward them as they were unearthed from their homes.

"So," said Daniel, scooping out a handful of dirt. "What's the plan once we get outta here?"

Carol hesitated; she knew Daniel wasn't going to like what she was about to say, but there really wasn't any other option. "I think we need to get back to camp and call the police. There's no way we can stay here and fight these guys."

"Wait!" exclaimed Daniel, standing and brushing his hand on his pants. "We leave? Didn't you hear them? They're going to be leaving soon, and that means they're going to be taking the birds with them."

"Yes, I know," argued Carol. "But there's no way we could take them all on. Plus, they could have guns, and I'd rather put off dying for another year or two."

"However," added Ava, "none of that is going to matter if you don't get back down here and help me dig."

"Fine," said Daniel, clearly displeased with the way things were going.

"I'm sorry," said Carol, helping to clear away another pile of dirt. "We've gotta make smart decisions."

Daniel continued digging, pretending not to hear her.

"I can see light," said Ava excitedly. She leaned forward and scooped another armful of dirt away from the back wall. "One sec...stop digging."

She dropped to her belly, twisted her head, and peered through the small hole they'd scooped out.

"What do you see?" whispered Carol.

"It looks like a tarp or something. Daniel, hand me my digging tool." Seconds later, she felt the cool metal in the palm of her hand. She rotated her body, laying on one side, and pushed her arm through the small opening. *Yep, it's a tarp.* She slid the strip of metal beneath the tarp and raised it a couple inches.

Franco and Raul were just stepping into their quarters. Raul turned and looked directly at Ava. *Please don't see me. Please don't see me.* She lay completely still, and then she saw Franco's meaty arm shoot out of the doorway and pull him inside.

Ava let out a sigh of relief, and then slowly backed out of the hole, wiping dirt and sweat from her eyes. "They just went inside. If we're going to get out, we'd better do it now!"

"All right," agreed Carol. "I don't have to be told twice. Let's do this."

"I'll go first," said Daniel. He lay on the ground and pulled himself forward. "See you on the other side."

"Be careful," whispered Ava. "Use the tarp for cover if you need to."

Daniel didn't answer. He wriggled his body forward like a lizard until he completely disappeared.

19

MAYHEM

Ava drooped down to her stomach. The moist dirt felt cool on her skin. Using her entire body, she pushed and pulled herself into the narrow opening. *Where's Daniel?* She'd expected him to be waiting for her behind the tarp.

Ava twisted, pulling her legs through the hole. She repositioned herself and helped Carol through. Carol's heart sank when she realized Daniel wasn't there.

Ava saw her expression and nodded. "I hope he doesn't do anything stupid," she whispered quietly.

Suddenly, the door to the trappers' headquarters swung open with a bang. Ava pulled the tarp open enough for her and Carol to peek out. Raul cupped his hands and lit a cigarette. He coughed loudly, sending a huge plume of smoke skyward.

"That's so disgusting," whispered Carol.

Raul took another long drag off his cigarette, turned toward the door, and stopped. A loud squawking noise erupted from the large metal building housing the birds.

Ava shared a look of dread with Carol. *Daniel is trying to free the animals.*

"Franco! Gustavo!"

"He's going to get us killed," said Carol angrily.

"We've got to get out of here!"

"How? We can't just go running through the jungle," Carol exclaimed.

"Follow me!" Ava flung the tarp back and raced toward an army jeep parked in front of the headquarters. She could hear Carol panting behind her.

"Get in!" waved Ava. "Get in!"

Carol jumped into the front seat, staring wide-eyed at Ava. "Do you even know how to—"

Ava twisted the key and stomped on the gas. The engine roared to life. She stomped on the gas again. The engine roared, but the jeep didn't move.

"You've gotta move that stick!" yelled Carol.

Gustavo appeared in the doorway of the headquarters, holding a rifle.

"Ava!" screamed Carol. "He's got a gun!"

Ava yanked backwards on the gear shift and stomped on the gas. The jeep lurched to life and then sped backwards, crashing into the poachers' house and sending Gustavo diving for safety. The horribly constructed sheet metal house wobbled, and part of the roof sagged and then caved in.

"Push the stick forward!" cried Carol. "Push the stick forward!"

"I'm trying!" yelled Ava through gritted teeth. She pushed forward on the gearshift, and it replied by making a screeching metallic sound. Ava pressed the gas and the jeep shot forward, crashing into a large crate.

Raul and Franco jumped in front of the jeep, machetes raised—but they were no match for Ava's crazed driving. At the last second, they dove to the ground, rolling away from the jeep.

"I think I'm getting the hang of it!" shouted Ava as she mowed over a motorcycle and slammed into the corner of the shed where they'd been held captive.

"Could you possibly try to drive without hitting something?" yelped Carol, hanging onto her seat for dear life.

"There's Daniel!" yelled Ava, tugging at the steering wheel. "I'm gonna swing by and get him."

"You mean run over him!" howled Carol.

"Please, I've got this," blurted Ava, running through a clothesline, barely missing the Bull's tighty-whities, and crashing through another row of wooden crates, sending them flying in all directions. Ava twisted the wheel hard and drove straight toward the building with the macaws.

Carol searched frantically for a seatbelt. Unfortunately, all she found was another dirty sock and a rusted can of wasp spray. She put both feet on the dash and pushed herself hard against her seat.

"Stop!" screamed Daniel, running through the open doorway, waving his arms above his head. Half a dozen macaws flew through the doors, screeching and cawing as they flew to freedom.

Ava slammed on the brakes, and the jeep slid sideways in the soft soil, kicking up a cloud of dirt and debris.

"Get in!" demanded Ava.

Carol spun in her seat and grabbed Daniel by the shirt, yanking him into the jeep. Franco the Bull appeared behind them.

"Go!" screamed Carol. "Go!"

But it was too late. Franco lifted the back of the jeep off the ground. "Boss!" he groaned. "I've got them!"

Ava stomped on the gas, but to no avail. Franco laughed as the back wheels spun helplessly in the air, the veins in his neck bulging like steel cables.

Raul and Gustavo were closing in! Daniel grabbed a rake from the back of the jeep and began jabbing Franco in the forehead.

"I'm going to kill you, little man!" yelled Franco.

"Ava, what are you doing?" gasped Daniel. "Put the jeep in reverse!"

"It's on the *R*," yelled Carol. "Isn't that reverse?"

"Put it on the *4*, for four-wheel drive!" shouted Daniel, releasing another volley of jabs.

Ava shifted the gear to four-wheel drive. Instantly, she felt the front tires dig in. Franco also had an instant realization: he realized he was about to be flattened. He released the bumper and dove to the side. The jeep hit the ground, fishtailed, and then slammed into a large pole.

"Forward!" yelled Carol and Daniel.

"Incoming!" cried Franco, as the large pole smashed to the ground beside him. The clothesline whipped through the air, sending Franco's giant tighty-whities airborne, only to be caught on the jeep's antenna. Carol watched, horrified, as they flapped in the wind like a giant flag.

Gustavo grabbed Ava's door and yanked it open. Ava slammed the gearshift forward just as Gustavo grabbed her hoodie.

"Gotcha!" he yelled.

Ava slammed her foot on the gas pedal. The jeep surged forward, accelerating, but Gustavo wouldn't let go. Carol grabbed Ava's other shoulder, engaging in an Ava tug-of-war as they dragged Gustavo across the campsite.

Daniel rose to his knees, thrust the rake at Gustavo, missed, and popped Ava upside the head.

"Dude," yelled Ava. "What the heck!"

Still clutching Ava's shoulder, Carol's fingers searched the floorboards of the jeep. "Yes!" She leaned forward and unleashed a full blast of wasp spray into Gustavo's face.

He screamed and arched his body backward to avoid the spray. Carol thought for sure he was going to let go, but the wasp spray only seemed to enrage the man.

"Carol!" shouted Ava, without turning her head. "I've got a plan."

"What is it?!" Carol cried out.

"Hang on!" screamed Ava.

"You'll tell me later?" yelled Carol.

"No, I mean *hold on*!"

Ava's knuckles turned white. Carol's face turned white. Daniel screamed in falsetto.

Ava gritted her teeth and pointed the jeep directly at the river. The wheels dug in, and it picked up speed as it raced toward the water.

"Ava!" Carol cried out. "We'll never make it!"

Gustavo recognized crazy when he saw it, and now he saw it in Ava's eyes. He screamed and let go of her, rolling away from the jeep like a log down a hill.

The jeep rocketed off the embankment, flying like a spectacular green rocket through the air. Just as Ava thought they were going to make it, the jeep plummeted, splashing down into the river. Carol shook her head and patted her body to see if she was still alive.

Daniel had flipped out of his seat and was balled up against the tailgate, entangled in Franco's underwear. He clambered to his hands and knees and shook his head. "Gross," he moaned, flinging the tighty-whities into the river.

"Hey!" yelled Franco. "That's my underwear!"

Everyone stopped for a moment to watch the gargantuan, white unmentionables float downstream.

"I've got two words for you!" Ava yelled at the men. "Caimans, leeches, and deadly snakes! The river's filled with them!"

"That's three," said Carol.

"Oh, yeah, three things, so even more dangerous!" Ava warned.

Franco and Raul turned to their boss, seeking guidance. "Don't listen to her, you idiots," screamed Gustavo. "Get them!"

Franco didn't hesitate. The behemoth man leaped from the embankment, tucked into a cannonball, and splashed into the water.

In any other situation, Ava would have applauded and held up a small sign that read 10. However, Franco ruined the moment when he resurfaced, screaming like a wild banshee and thrusting his fist into the air.

"Go!" yelled Ava. "Go!" She and Carol scampered to the hood of the jeep and dove into the water, racing to the opposite shore.

Ava reached the other side first and clambered onto the muddy beach. She pushed her hair out of her eyes with the side of her hand and immediately looked for her friends.

"They got Daniel," groaned Carol, pulling herself from the water.

For the second time that day, Daniel was thrown over Franco's shoulder. He must have been angry about his underwear because Franco held him by the ankles and dragged him through the water. Daniel had to fight to keep his head from being submerged. Gustavo smiled cruelly at them and offered his hand to Franco, pulling him up the embankment.

"Why isn't Franco chasing us?" Ava was interrupted by the roaring of a motorcycle engine, racing toward the embankment.

"He's gonna try to jump!" yelled Carol.

"Didn't he see what happened to us?" asked Ava incredulously. "He's not gonna make it."

Then, as if by magic, the man seemingly did the impossible. He "flew" across the river, and then whipped his bike toward the girls.

"A suspension bridge," gasped Carol, pointing. "They had a bridge!"

Ava followed Carol's finger. A narrow bridge camouflaged with vines and branches spanned the river. "How did I not see that?"

"There's no time to second-guess ourselves. Come on!"

The motorcycle tore along the shoreline, its engine growling like a demonic beast. Carol and Ava sprinted through the jungle, tripping over roots and vines. Both girls had the same thought: at this speed, running blindly through the jungle, they risked the chance of running into a venomous spider or a deadly viper.

Carol felt for the tiny button on her survival band and flicked the flashlight on. The risk of not knowing where they were going was too great. They needed light to help guide their way. Unfortunately, it made them an easy target for their pursuer to follow.

"He's gaining on us," gasped Ava.

"I know," Carol panted. "But I've got a plan!"

"I'm all ears," Ava puffed, narrowly dodging a banana tree.

***

Carol crouched in the darkness, hidden behind a clump of underbrush. The angry roar of the motorcycle grew closer. The girls could see the headlight slicing through the darkness. Ava waited until she was sure Raul saw her. Then she spun around and took off running through the jungle, screaming. The ground shook as he pulled back on the throttle and shot after her.

Carol exhaled and waited till the last second. She jumped to her feet and yanked hard on a vine she'd tied to a tree on the other side of the path. Raul screamed as the vine caught him across his chest, sending him flying through the air. He landed heavily on his back with an "oof."

Carol immediately rushed to him and slammed her heel into his solar plexus. A gasp escaped his helmet, and then he lay still. She reached into his pocket and grabbed his phone. *Probably has all kinds of evidence on it.*

Ava slid to a stop beside Carol. "It worked!"

"Tie him up before he comes to!"

Ava pulled the string from her hoodie and quickly tied his feet together. She yanked his boots off and stripped them of their laces.

"Let's flip him over," said Carol. "And tie his hands behind his back."

"Got it," said Ava.

The girls rolled him over onto his belly. Carol squeezed his arms tightly together while Ava used the shoelaces to bind his wrists. A moan came from inside his helmet. They rolled him onto his back. Ava released the clasp under Raul's chin and tugged his helmet off.

Raul's eyes burned with anger. He spat out a flurry of words Ava and Carol didn't understand—and were pretty sure they didn't want to. He struggled, trying to break free.

"Keep moving," said Carol bitterly, "and I'm going to give you another heel stomp! Understood?" She raised her foot above his chest to make her point.

Raul cursed again. "When I get free, I'm going to kill you both."

"Aw, Raul, see, you shouldn't have said that," said Ava, returning with the leather satchel from his motorcycle. She turned it over and dumped the contents onto the ground. She grabbed a roll of duct tape. "Perfect."

Raul eyed the roll of tape and then began screaming, "Help! Help!"

"He obviously speaks the universal language of duct tape." Ava tore off a strip and then placed it over his mouth. "Much better," she sighed.

"You better put on another piece," said Carol. "Just in case."

"My pleasure," smiled Ava, adding another piece of tape over his mouth. She kicked around the items she'd dumped on the ground from Raul's satchel. She grabbed a pocketknife and a coil of rope. "What do we do with him?" asked Ava. "We can't just leave him here. He'll become somebody's dinner."

Raul nodded his head. The hatred had been replaced with fear.

"Well," smiled Carol. "I guess we'll have to do what we do when we go camping, so scavengers don't get our food."

Ava shrugged her shoulders. "Put him in a cooler?" Carol made a face. "What? I have no idea what you're talking about."

"May I?" Carol took the bundle of rope from Ava, uncoiled it, tied a loop in one end, and then heaved it over a large tree limb about ten feet off the ground.

"Oh," nodded Ava. "I see, great idea."

The girls dragged Raul by his feet under the tree. He shook his head back and forth, his eyes wide with fear.

"Don't worry," Carol said brightly. "You're gonna be fine." She ran the rope beneath his belt, knotted it in place, and then stepped back. "All right, Aves, pull!"

The girls wrapped the end of the rope around their wrists and leaned backwards. Raul's body jerked upward. "Heave," gasped Carol. For such a thin man, he was certainly heavy. The girls dropped down, lowering their center of gravity, and pulled harder. Raul shot up another three feet. They repeated the series: drop, pull, drop, pull, until he dangled from his belt, eight feet in the air. Carol wrapped the rope around another tree, and then tied it off.

"Nicely done," smiled Carol, wiping the sweat from her forehead. "Now we just need to get back to camp and get help. We could take his motorcycle," she suggested.

"About that," said Ava. "If we go all the way back to camp, by the time we get back, they'll most likely be gone, and who knows what they'll do to Daniel. These guys aren't playing." Ava motioned to Raul's motorcycle. A rifle was strapped to its side.

Carol hesitated. "I don't know if we can do this by ourselves. They're expecting us to go to the police and get help."

"Yes, exactly, which is why they won't be ready for us," argued Ava. "They think we're long gone. They're going to be focusing on loading up the boat and clearing out of the camp."

"I don't know...."

"Yes, you do. They won't expect us to reappear, and that's why we have the advantage. Plus, we can't risk them hurting Daniel...it would destroy his mother."

"You know how to get to me, don't you? You had to bring up his mother. All right," agreed Carol. "I'm in." She turned and looked at Raul, who was gently swinging in the breeze. "And just in case he somehow gets loose...." She walked over to the motorcycle, removed the keys from the ignition, and then, kneeling beside the engine, ripped out a handful of colorful wires. "That should do the trick."

"Beautiful work, inspiring. Should we set it on fire?" asked Ava. "I feel like we should set it on fire."

"Maybe next time. Come on, Ava, we've got to rescue Daniel."

20

A DARING RESCUE

Carol and Ava lay on their stomachs, watching the campsite from the suspension bridge. Gustavo and Franco were hurriedly carrying cages to the floating pallets connected to the back of the speedboat.

"I knew it," whispered Ava. "They're making a break for it."

"Yep. And I don't see Daniel anywhere."

"Me either," said Ava, her voice tinged with worry. "My best guess is the building where they're keeping the birds, so they can keep an eye on him—"

"Or the shed," suggested Carol. "Most likely they tied him up this time." *Or worse,* she thought. She couldn't bring herself to say the words.

"Okay," nodded Ava. "Let's check the shed first. Our top priority is rescuing Daniel, then the birds."

"Agreed," nodded Carol.

The girls army crawled the length of the bridge. From their vantage point, they were completely hidden.

"As soon as they go into the building to get more cages, we go," whispered Carol.

Ava nodded in agreement, keeping her eyes focused on the two men.

"Now!" Ava and Carol sprinted to the shed and crouched down, leaning their backs against the steel wall. "It's locked," whispered Carol.

Ava crept over to the front door of the shed. A thick metal clasp was secured by a padlock. "No way we're getting that thing off, unless you found a crowbar in Raul's pocket."

"Wait," said Carol excitedly. She fished around in her pocket. "I didn't find a crowbar, but I did find these." She pulled out a keyring. "They were in the motorcycle ignition."

Ava took the keys from Carol. "Good job!" She flipped through the keys on the keychain. "It's gotta be this one." She held the lock steady, pushed the key inside, and twisted. The lock sprang open. "And...we're in," Ava smiled, wiggling her eyebrows.

"I'll keep an eye out for Franco and Gustavo. You get Daniel."

Ava slowly opened the door to the shed. "Daniel?" she called out softly.

Daniel sat hunched over against the back wall, his head slumped forward, his chin on his chest. His arms and legs were bound tightly.

"Daniel," said Ava softly. "It's me, Ava. Are you okay?"

It took a moment for Daniel to realize what was happening. He shook his head as if waking up from a dream.

Ava gasped when she saw his face. His right eye was swollen shut. His bottom lip was twice its normal size, and dried blood was caked on his chin and the corners of his mouth.

"What did they do to you? Are you okay?" The words caught in her throat.

"You came back," he whispered hoarsely. He tried to smile, but winced instead.

"Of course we came back. We're not in the habit of leaving our friends behind." She hurried over, pulled the pocketknife she'd found in Raul's satchel from her pocket, and sawed through the ropes.

"Thank you," said Daniel, his voice cracking with emotion. He looked at his arms. Deep grooves encircled his wrists. He opened and closed his hands with great effort. "They're numb," he explained.

Carol's face appeared in the doorway. "We need to get going!"

"One second," said Ava. She slid around behind Daniel and helped him to his feet.

"Can you walk?" She stood behind him in case he fell backward.

"Yeah," he said, standing on wobbly legs. "Sorry. They tied the ropes so tight, my hands and feet went numb."

Carol stepped into the doorway again to hurry them along, but when she saw Daniel's face, her mouth clamped shut. Anger filled her eyes.

"Why did they beat you? You're just a kid," Carol cried.

"I think Gustavo has anger issues. I'm fine, guys. It looks a lot worse than it is."

"Not so sure about that," said Ava, making a face. "You look like you got in a fight with a baseball bat and lost. Badly."

Carol checked on Gustavo and Franco the Bull. "They're still loading up the boat."

"So," Daniel said, his face filling with determination. "What's the plan?"

"The plan? The plan was to rescue you and then to get help," explained Carol.

"No." Daniel stomped his foot like a child. "We can't let them get away! Then all of this will have been for nothing."

Carol wheeled on Daniel. "You're in no shape to do anything. What you need is medical attention. Plus, what are we supposed to do? Wreck their boat?"

A huge smile filled Ava's face. "Yes, please, I'm actually great at wrecking things."

Daniel disappeared into the shed and returned with a thick rusty chain, twice the length of his body. "I have a better idea."

"Are you sure it will work?" Ava asked.

"Wait a minute, Daniel, for real. You're not in any shape to do this."

"I'm fine, really. It was just a couple punches, okay? Now let's do this!"

"All right," said Ava, turning to Carol. "We've fought against crazy odds before."

"Okay, Daniel," Carol smiled. "What's your plan?"

"It's simple. Just help me get the chain down to the boat, and I'll take care of the rest."

"As soon as I say go," Carol said, watching Gustavo and the Bull, "run like your pants are on fire."

"Oh," said Daniel, turning to Ava and handing her the other end of the heavy chain. "Please try to keep up."

"They're walking toward the bird building—they're going inside.... Go!" Carol whispered urgently.

Ava and Daniel rushed down to the boat, the heavy chain swinging back and forth between them. If Daniel was in pain, it didn't show. He slid down the embankment by the dock, pulling Ava down with him.

They froze at the bottom of the ravine. The site of the caged parrots on the floating pallet was horrific. The caged birds squawked and screeched, frightened and in pain. Daniel looked at his wrists. The deep channels were raw where the rope had bit into his skin. He wanted to fling the cages open and set the birds free, but in his heart, he knew that he needed to put an end to this.

"I'm sorry," he whispered. "You will be free soon. I promise." He turned to Ava. "Help me with the chain." Together they lifted it over his head. It hung over his shoulders like a scarf.

"I'll be right back. Keep an eye out." Without another word, he waded into the water and disappeared behind the boat.

Ava climbed up the embankment and lay on the ground. Gustavo and Franco were still in the main building about seventy-five feet away. Across the campsite, she could see Carol crouched behind the shed. Ava smiled to herself. There was no doubt that her best friend was plotting and planning.

Franco appeared in the doorway, his arms stacked with cages. Gustavo was struggling with a gas-powered generator. She slid down to the water. Daniel had been underwater for over a minute. *Where is he?*

She could hear the men's voices. She crawled back up the embankment and peeked over the edge. The two men had stopped to trade loads. Franco handed the cages to Gustavo, and then he picked up the generator like he was picking up a feather.

Ava slid and then jumped down to the shore just as Daniel's head surfaced. "They're coming, they're coming," she whispered urgently, motioning for him to get out of the water.

Daniel pointed to a clump of vegetation, just beyond the dock. Ava nodded and scurried over. Daniel swam like a frog, not making a sound, and then climbed out of the water onto the shore, just as Franco appeared.

"Oh my God," said Ava, as Daniel hurried over. "You have a leech…. Oh, never mind, it was just your lip."

"Funny," he whispered. He took a look at the boat and shook his head. "Unless they have another engine somewhere, that boat isn't going anywhere."

"Awesome," said Ava excitedly. "Now all we need to do is call the police!"

"How?" asked Daniel. "They took our phones."

"Yeah, and we took Raul's," she smiled.

"Wait…I haven't seen Raul." He smiled painfully. "Where is he?"

"Oh," whispered Ava nonchalantly. "He's hanging around."

21

THE CHASE

Daniel and Ava rejoined Carol behind the shed.

"How did it go?" Carol asked anxiously.

"Perfect," Ava said. "Do you have that phone?"

"Yeah." Carol dug in her pocket and handed Daniel the phone.

"It's a flip phone," he said, frowning.

"Yeah...and?"

"It's just that the signal...." Daniel pressed the button on the side and waited. "Yep," he sighed. "No signal. It's probably why they have all those antennas. They must have a radio receiver." He handed the phone back to Carol.

"So now what do we do, Big Brain?"

"Hang on, I'm working on that." Carol peeked around the shed. Franco was cradling a car battery and two incubators. Gustavo had an armful of equipment as well.

"Okay," said Carol, turning to Ava and Daniel. "As soon as they get to the boat, we find the radio and call for help. It's our only chance."

Franco carefully maneuvered down the slope to the boat, balancing the incubators. Gustavo followed at his heels. "Watch it! Watch it! Those birds are worth a fortune."

Unseen, the trio bolted from behind the shed and raced across the campsite to the trappers' building. Ava threw open the door and stepped inside. "Ugh," she grimaced. "It smells like sweaty socks in here."

The sheet metal building consisted of one giant room. Three sleeping bags lay on the floor beside a table with a coffeemaker and two propane grills. Several gallon jugs of water were stacked in the corner.

"There," said Daniel, pointing to a wooden table. "The radio!"

"Oh," whispered Carol. "How the heck do you work this thing?" The radio had dozens of buttons and knobs, none of which made any sense to her.

Ava pressed the power button, and the digital readout came to life. "Twenty-one, dot, two, nine, five, dot, zero, zero. Does that mean anything to anyone?"

"It must be some kind of frequency," Carol suggested.

"And this must be the microphone," said Ava, picking up a small oval handpiece that was connected by a coiled wire to the radio. She pressed the button on the side. "Breaker, breaker, come in!"

"What the heck are you doing?" asked Daniel.

"I don't know," Ava shrugged. "I saw it on a movie once with a bunch of truck drivers."

"Maybe you need to be wearing the headphones," said Daniel.

"Oh, yeah." She slipped them over her head and rotated the large black knob beneath the display. The digital numbers changed. There was a blast of static in the headphones, and then Ava could hear people talking.

"Keep turning it," Daniel encouraged.

"No! No!" Ava smacked his hand away from the dial. "I hear voices! Hello? Hello? Anyone there?"

Suddenly from outside there was a loud explosion, followed by angry screams. Daniel turned and looked at Carol. His not-swollen eye flew open wide. "The boat!"

"Ava," Carol yelled. "Keep trying—we'll be right back."

Daniel and Carol raced to the door. Gustavo and Franco clambered up the embankment into the camp. "It must have been the kid," Gustavo screamed, pointing at the shed. "Bring me that kid!"

Daniel and Carol jerked back from the doorway, but it was too late. Gustavo had seen them. Carol dashed across the room.

"Mayday, Mayday!" yelled Ava into the microphone.

Carol ripped the headphones from Ava's head, sending them crashing to the floor. "They're coming!"

Daniel spun in a circle in the center of the room. There was only one way out. He grabbed a gallon jug of water, ran to the door, and waited. Just as Gustavo flung the door open, Daniel hurled the water jug, smacking him in the face. Gustavo fell backwards, sprawling on the ground. "Franco!" he screamed. "Kill them!"

The young trio burst through the door. "The bridge!" yelled Carol.

They sprinted across the campsite, but Franco cut them off. A huge smile crossed his face. "Want to race to the bridge?"

"Wanna sing soprano?" yelled Ava.

For a mountain of a man, he was incredibly fast. He unsheathed a nasty curved knife and sprinted toward them. "Cowards!"

Gustavo raced toward them from the other direction, hoping to cut them off.

"Run directly toward Gustavo," puffed Ava. "Make it look like we're going to attack him. At the last second, break right, and I'll break left. Meet up behind their headquarters!"

"Got it!" Daniel and Carol spun around and lowered their shoulders, running straight at Gustavo. He dug his heels in, bracing for the attack. Behind them, they could hear Franco's footsteps pounding, getting closer.

Daniel snarled, throwing out his arms like he was going to tackle Gustavo. Gustavo planted his feet and crouched. At the last second, Daniel and Carol cut right, and Ava cut left, sprinting past him. Franco bent over behind them, hands on his knees, panting.

"Give me that!" screamed Gustavo, snatching the knife from Franco's hand.

"We can't run from them forever," Ava gasped. "We're going to have to separate them and then take them down, one by one."

"I hate to say it," Carol panted, "but you're right. Franco can barely breathe right now," she pointed out. "If we can lure Gustavo into the jungle, we may have a chance."

"Leave that to me," said Ava, stepping from her hiding place, behind the villains' headquarters. "Oh, Gustavo," she taunted. "You better hurry and get out of here. We radioed the police. They'll be here any minute."

"Oh, really?" he sneered. "That's a receiver. You can't radio anyone."

"Oh, really," taunted Ava. "Because it seems to have a microphone, and I'm pretty sure they heard me. Carol, throw me Raul's phone. And thanks to this…."

"What's that?" asked Gustavo, creeping closer.

"Oh, this little thing?" Ava held up her hand. "It's Raul's phone. Think of all the evidence on it."

"Where's Raul? How did you get his phone?" Gustavo demanded.

"He told us to tell you he won't be able to come to work today. He's a little tied up at the moment."

Gustavo's face turned bright red. He looked like he was about to erupt. "You little…." He raised the knife above his head and rushed at the children, slashing wildly.

Ava, Carol, and Daniel turned and sprinted through the jungle. Daniel led, and the girls stuck to him like glue. A knife whizzed past Carol's head, disappearing into the trees.

"Stop!" screamed Gustavo. "Or I promise you, the next one won't miss."

"The game is over," said Ava. "You lost." Daniel and Carol stood on either side of her. "Soon this place is going to be crawling with police. Throw down your knife and give up."

Gustavo smiled and then spat at Ava's feet. "You know what?" He gestured with his knife. "I think you're a liar. No one is coming. I'm going to tie you to a log, and then I'm going to watch as Franco hurls you into the river." He smiled, envisioning the thought. "You're going to hope that you drown, because I hear that being eaten by a caiman is a slow, painful death."

"You forget that there's three of us, and we won't go down easily."

"I'm giving you punks one last chance," growled Gustavo. "Think about it. Maybe you'll get lucky and someone will rescue you from the log before you die…. Or you can die right now."

"You're pitiful," sneered Ava. "I faced down bigger bullies than you in preschool."

"Maybe you're right. Maybe I should let you go, and just throw away half a million dollars." He grinned evilly and then lashed out wildly at Daniel, who jumped backwards, slamming into a tree. Cupuacu fruit—the size of coconuts—rained down onto him. He rolled away and leaped to his feet.

"You're a quick one," laughed Gustavo, closing in on him. He leaped forward, thrusting the knife at Daniel again and narrowly missing him. The blade sank deep into the tree.

Ava and Carol charged him, slamming into his midsection with their shoulders. Gustavo fell to the ground, kicking and punching. His foot lashed out and caught Carol in the stomach. She cried out and fell to the ground in a ball, gasping for air.

"Ava, get the knife!" screamed Daniel. He dove on top of Gustavo, punching and clawing.

Ava grabbed the knife and pulled, but it was buried deep in the tree. She grabbed the handle, moving the knife up and down, trying to work it loose.

Daniel screamed out as he took a brutal elbow to his jaw. He sprawled on the ground, shaking his head dizzily. Gustavo jumped to his feet. Wasting no time, he charged into Ava, sending her crashing onto a rotting log. Stars filled her vision as she fought for air.

Gustavo clutched the knife with both hands—he put his foot on the tree for leverage and pulled. The weapon slid out of the tree with a sickening slippery sound. Gustavo's eyes were crazed. Blood ran from his lips and nose. He whirled around and clucked his tongue.

"Pitiful," he growled.

"Yes, yes, you are," said Ava, clutching her side. "You thought that was all we've got? That was just a warm-up."

"Oh, really?" sneered the man. "Then I think it's time for the final play." He flipped his knife from one hand to the other.

"Hey, Gustavo!" yelled Daniel. "Do you like fresh fruit?"

Daniel whipped his hand in a quick circle and then flipped it toward Gustavo. A brown circular object hit the tree beside Gustavo and exploded into fragments of white and brown. Gustavo tripped over a root, and before he could completely recover, Daniel had reloaded his sock sling and launched another Cupuacu fruit at his head.

This one hit its mark. A look of bewilderment filled Gustavo's face as he stumbled backwards and fell to the ground. The knife slipped from his fingertips and dropped beside him.

Carol rushed over and kicked the knife away. It wasn't until that moment that Ava realized Carol was missing a sock. "Oh," Ava smiled, looking from her to Daniel. "The sling!"

Daniel nodded. "The perfect weapon." Ava and Carol grabbed Gustavo's arms, and Daniel slipped his belt off and tied Gustavo's wrists together.

Carol wrestled off one of Gustavo's boots and yanked the shoelace out. She wrapped it around his legs twice and then tied a knot.

"I'll never make fun of your jumbo socks again," smiled Ava.

Gustavo shook his head, slowly coming to. "You filthy pieces of...."

"If I may." Daniel picked up Carol's sock and stuffed it into Gustavo's mouth.

22

FRANCO THE BULL

Carol and Daniel dragged Gustavo to a tree and tied him to it with a piece of vine.

"Don't worry," said Ava, patting Gustavo's head. "We'll come back and get you in a couple days.... If there's anything left of you."

Gustavo shook his body from side to side, trying to break free, his eyes a mixture of fear and anger.

"All right," said Carol, rubbing her hands together. "Two down, one more to go."

The trio crept quietly through the jungle. A thought kept nagging Carol. *Why didn't Franco come to help his boss? Maybe he believed Ava's lie about the police?*

Daniel threw up his hand, stopping them. "I hear them too," whispered Ava. "Voices." They dropped to their hands and knees and crawled to a downed tree. A thin man dressed in camouflage with a rifle slung over his back came into view.

"Oh, great," whispered Carol. "Is that Raul?"

Suddenly Daniel leaped to his feet.

Carol looked up at him, shocked. "Daniel!" she yelled, but it was too late. He raced across the campsite. The man in black spun toward him, tearing his rifle from his shoulder. He pointed it at Daniel and yelled, "Stop!"

Suddenly a tiny woman holding a frying pan came into view. She shoved the man with the rifle aside and threw open her arms. "Daniel!" she cried.

Ava and Carol shared a look of bewilderment. What had just happened?

Daniel turned and pointed to where the girls were hiding. Suddenly, Miquel and Marcia appeared. "Ava! Carol!" they screamed, racing to them.

The girls leaped to their feet. Miquel crashed into Ava and threw his arms around her, lifting her into the air.

Marcia embraced Carol. Tears streamed down her cheeks. "You're okay," she whispered. She held Carol's shoulders, searching her eyes.

"I'm good. We're okay, Marcia."

"How did you find us?" asked Ava, her mind reeling.

"When Daniel's mother checked his room this morning," said Marcia.

Morning? The word sounded so absurd to Carol. She tilted her eyes skyward. *Yep, it's morning.*

"She realized Daniel was missing. She remembered him talking with you and Ava, so we checked your cabin. We knew he must have been with you. Thankfully, Sanchez is an amazing tracker, and he led us here."

Ava and Carol followed Marcia and Miquel over to the others. Sanchez was sitting on Franco the Bull's stomach, smoking a cigarette.

He took a look at the girls' disheveled clothes and cuts and bruises and nodded. It was one of Ava's proudest moments, seeing the profound thanks and respect in his eyes.

She returned a subtle nod, and then embraced Daniel's mother, who reached out and grabbed Carol. She pulled her in, giving them both a bone-crushing hug.

"You guys got Franco the Bull," smiled Ava.

"Yes," nodded Miquel, laughing. "Not quite sure which scared him the most, Rebecca's frying pan or Sanchez's rifle."

"Definitely the frying pan," moaned Franco.

A deep hum emanated from the river. Moments later, a sleek silver boat with the word *Polícia* on it appeared in the Cobra Pequena. Daniel turned to the girls and hugged them. "We got them," Daniel smiled.

"Yeah," said Carol, tussling his wet hair. "We got them."

23
FAREWELL

Ava walked across Dead-man's crossing without a second thought. It seemed like eons ago when she had been afraid to pass over the chasm. The trip had taught her a lot about herself. She'd learned to face her fears. She'd learned that there were much bigger problems out there—much worse than horrible soap, or her green hair. There were living beings out there that needed protection because they couldn't protect themselves.

She had also learned how fear could be used as a weapon—and how a simple tale about a Red Devil had paralyzed an entire village for generations. Lastly, she realized the lengths that people will go when they feel the need to fight against what they feel is unjust. She glanced at her wrist, where a simple hand-woven bracelet lay. A gift from Daniel's mother.

Ava stood at the end of the bridge and looked behind her. The chasm far below was now familiar to her. The sounds of the rainforest were no longer a chaotic cacophony of sound, but a simple beautiful melody, created by individual beings—each perfect in their own unique way.

Miquel, Marcia, Daniel, Rebecca, and Juliana stood at the other side of the bridge. She turned, raised her hands to her chest, and moved her fingers into the shape of a heart. She would always carry these memories with her. Her new friends returned the simple gesture. A lump formed in her throat.

She stepped off the swaying bridge, threw her arm around Carol's shoulder, and smiled.

Carol looked back at her brightly, her blue eyes sparkling in the sunlight.

"I know what you're thinking," Ava whispered, hugging her best friend against her. "You can't believe Elliot turned out to be a girl."

New Book Releases and Companion Guide

Thank you for reading The Curse of the Red Devil, seventh book of the Ava & Carol Detective Agency series! Sign up for our newsletter and download the free PDF file of the "Rainforest Animal Guide" at avaandcarol.com/rainforest.php

You may also follow Thomas Lockhaven's author page on Amazon or Bookbub for new release updates.

If you enjoyed the book, please leave a review on Amazon, Goodreads, or Barnes & Noble. We'd love to hear from you! Thank you so much for reading our book, we are incredibly grateful!

Be sure to check out our other exciting books in the action-packed series.

Ava & Carol Detective Agency

Book 1: The Mystery of the Pharaoh's Diamonds
Book 2: The Mystery of Solomon's Ring
Book 3: The Haunted Mansion
Book 4: Dognapped
Book 5: The Eye of God
Book 6: The Crown Jewels Mystery
Book 7: The Curse of the Red Devil

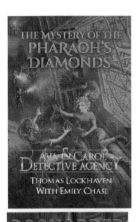  

Upcoming titles

Book 8: The Shakespeare Heist (Upcoming)
Book 9: The Secret at Shadow Creek (Upcoming)

Extra 1: Ava & Carol Detective Agency: Rainforest Animal Guide (Upcoming) – Companion guide to The Curse of the Red Devil
Extra 2: Ava & Carol Detective Agency Handbook (Upcoming)

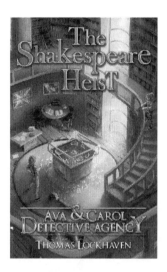
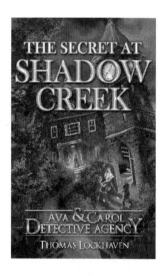

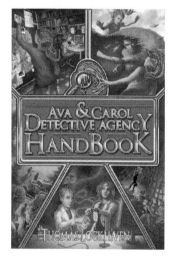

Others by Thomas Lockhaven

Quest Chasers series

Book 1: The Deadly Cavern
Book 2: The Screaming Mummy

The Ghosts of Ian Stanley series

The Ghosts of Ian Stanley: Book 1

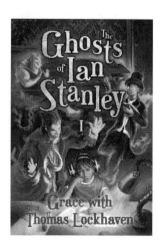

Made in the USA
Las Vegas, NV
23 October 2021